# Eastward in Eden

Books by Terence Faherty:

The Owen Keane Series

Deadstick (1991)
Live to Regret (1992)
The Lost Keats (1993)
Die Dreaming (1994)
Prove the Nameless (1996)
The Ordained (1997)
Orion Rising (1999)
Eastward in Eden (2013)

The Scott Elliott Series

Kill Me Again (1996)
Come Back Dead (1997)
Raise the Devil (2000)
In a Teapot (2005)
Dance in the Dark (2011)

Short fiction

The Confessions of Owen Keane (2005)
The Hollywood Op: Private Eye Scott Elliott in Tinseltown (2011)

# Eastward in Eden

*An Owen Keane Mystery*

Terence Faherty

The Mystery Company
*Mount Vernon, Ohio*

EASTWARD IN EDEN

Copyright © 2013 by Terence Faherty

ISBN-10: 1-932325-49-2
ISBN-13: 978-1-932325-49-2

Cover design by Pat Prather
Owen Keane image by Samuel Bayer

First published by The Mystery Company, an imprint of Crum Creek Press

First edition: October 2013

Crum Creek Press / The Mystery Company
1558 Coshocton Ave #126
Mount Vernon, OH 43050

www.crumcreekpress.com

*For Michael Wozniak*

# Eastward in Eden

## WALKING THE EDGE

I took a walk to clear my head after the long flight and found that it wouldn't clear. That is, I found that the flight wasn't the only problem, that jet lag wasn't the only problem. The fuzzy feeling between my ears also had to do with being on the opposite side of things. Of the world. Of my youth. Of the looking glass. No amount of exercise would cure that.

Still, I gave walking every chance. I set out on a circuit recommended by a bellman at the New Stanley. A little way east of the hotel, I picked up Moi Avenue and headed north to University Way. I made a left on University and followed it to the Uhuru Highway. To my right as I walked south was an irregular hedge of bright red bougainvillea and, beyond that, Uhuru Park, which I'd been told to avoid. For that reason alone, I was planning a visit. Sometime. Just then the park couldn't compete for my attention with the view to my left, the city center of Nairobi, Kenya.

The buildings grew in size as I walked but retained the boxy sixties style I'd noted as far back as University. I'd noted it with approval, quieting my nerves with the false idea that I'd changed decades rather than continents, that I'd moved through time to something familiar rather than through space to somewhere very unfamiliar. The convention center—a golden high-rise—and the government buildings around it were also dated and comforting. The Parliament building actually reminded me of my old high school, with an ornate clock tower stuck on to give it some height.

I checked my watch against the golden hands of the tower's clock. They agreed exactly. I couldn't remember switching from New Jersey time to East African time, but my memories of my arrival were already a jumble. Perhaps the stewardesses in the airliner's first class cabin had snuck around while we'd slept and reset our watches. The service had been that comprehensive.

The conspiracy between the tower clock and my Timex should have reinforced the fantasy that my surroundings were familiar, but it had the opposite effect. I began to note jarring details about the formerly homey Nairobi skyline, things I'd been editing out of the frame. Incredibly tall palm trees, for example, and—almost as graceful—the minarets of mosques. And I admitted to myself that my fellow pedestrians—growing in number as I continued south—were unlike any I'd walked among before. They wore simple but colorful clothing, long skirts, long sleeves, and long pants predominating despite the heat, making my traveling attire of white dress shirt and black trousers seem almost fashionable. The snatches of conversation I could hear above the traffic noise were also new, not only in their words, but in their accent and rhythm. Even the burdens the others carried were noteworthy: strange produce in long net bags and, here and there, chickens, alive but resigned to their fate. As I told myself I was.

I nodded to the people I passed and received nods and sometimes smiles in return, but no one spoke to me. This was surprising. I'd been warned by the friendly bellman that I'd be approached by itinerant tour guides, by street vendors, and possibly by prostitutes, all drawn to the very pale skin that marked me as a tourist newly arrived in the tropics. But this didn't happen.

It was as though the isolation I'd lived in for the past two years had followed me somehow to Africa. I'd thought that the isolation had been my own choice, stubbornly maintained. Now I was forced to consider another possibility. My long solitary state may have been something chosen for me by the people around me, a response to something about me, some mark or stain that even these strangers could see.

At the intersection of the highway and Haile Selassie Avenue I turned east to walk the leg that would bring me back to Moi Avenue and complete my circuit. But when I sighted Moi, I found I wasn't ready to stop walking. Though I'd left my guidebook and its handy maps back at the hotel, I decided to continue east. I could see a large ramshackle building ahead that turned out to be a bus terminal. Next to it was an open market, from which the calls of hawkers rose in a steady indecipherable noise, like a distant falsetto surf.

I skirted the market and, when its clamor had dropped away to nothing, I turned down a tree-lined, inviting street. I'd walked in its shade for a dusty block or two when the sound of screeching brakes drew my attention to an even smaller side street to my right.

The only building of any size on the side street was a brick church. It had battlements in place of a steeple, reminding me of older Methodist churches I'd seen in the Midwest. The van whose brakes I'd heard had pulled up directly in front of the building's steps.

An identical white van was already parked there, next to a tiny police cruiser of some Japanese make. As I started toward the church, its doors flew open and two helmeted policemen came out, dragging a struggling man between them. The man was wearing a clerical collar on a shirt of light gray. A second man in gray—not struggling—was escorted out by a second pair of policemen. I could hear voices inside the church, raised in angry protest.

Here it is, I thought, my earlier nervousness gone. This is my stop.

I was in the street, heading for the church, when my arm was seized from behind. I turned, expecting to see a policeman of my own, and found instead an elderly woman, her eyes wide with alarm in her dark upturned face. She tugged me back toward the grassy berm.

"Preacher, come away," she said. "Come away now. You don't want to go over there. There's nothing for you over there but trouble."

She didn't relax her grip on my arm until we were back on the shady street I'd followed from Haile Selassie. Then she said, "Sorry, Preacher. Sorry. But you should know better."

"I'm not a preacher," I said, thinking she had been misled by my clothes. She hadn't been.

"You're not?" the woman asked, dropping my arm. "Then God wasted the face of one when he made you. Those policemen won't believe you. They'll take one look at your preacher face and knock you on the head. You'll be a preacher then whether you want to be or not."

I heard one of the van doors slam shut, the sound a hollow jail-cell clang. "What's going on back there?" I asked.

"You really aren't a preacher," the woman said, convinced at last. "A preacher would know."

"Know what?"

"The pastor of that church spoke out against the government. Against the elections. So the police came to call."

Her words were chilling, but her matter-of-fact tone and her acceptance of the inevitability of cause and effect were more frightening still.

"It's not your fight, Mr. Tourist," she said, demoting me officially. "You go back where you belong. And you go quietly."

# CHAPTER ONE

"Mr. Owen Keane to see Director McKenzie."

The receptionist had repeated my request perfectly and she knew it, but she still waited for me to nod my approval before she reached for her phone. One last chance to change my mind.

It was June 1997. I was in Nairobi, Kenya, in the front office of a missionary society, the Crown Hill Society. Less than two weeks earlier I'd been happily ignorant of the group. Now I was standing on a worn spot of the society's jute floor covering, listening to the sounds of Nairobi traffic coming through its open windows.

The receptionist, an attractive woman who wore her hair in very soft, very tiny curls, reminded me of the young office workers I'd met the evening before in a bar across from the New Stanley Hotel. Friendly and talkative—on any subject except local politics—they'd been anxious to question me about America, about the latest trends, movies, and music. I was a poor source for that kind of information, but I'd tried my best, anxious for once for human interaction. The local beer had been good, too.

So good that I now had a headache to compete with my standard case of nerves. The receptionist seemed to sense this, almost whispering her glad tidings to me: "The director will see you right away."

McKenzie was a small, ferrety man whose very apparent nervousness relaxed me greatly. If only he'd had an obvious throbbing in his head, my own might have gone away. I smiled at that thought, and McKenzie smiled back. It was a disarming smile, revealing as it did a mouthful of extremely independent teeth, no two pointing in exactly the same direction.

He gestured me toward the most solid looking of his chairs, but I chose one farther from the open windows and the traffic noise. Before I was settled McKenzie was seated again himself and studying a tiny slip of paper which seemed to puzzle him. It turned out to be a record of the call I'd made from my hotel requesting the interview.

In a soft-edged Scottish accent, the director asked, "You're a friend of Father Swickard's, is that correct?"

A chance to lie right off the bat. I sidestepped it. "We were in the seminary together." And then, to forestall the obvious question. "I dropped out."

That ancient history, the defining act of my life, was neither here nor there to McKenzie, who still had his unruly teeth sunk in the current problem. "And you've come all the way from America to see him, to visit him, without letting him know that you were coming?"

"Yes." Something more was called for, so I said, "A mutual friend, a monk we knew in the seminary, who's been corresponding with Father Swickard all these years, asked me to make the trip. He's concerned about Father Swickard's welfare."

The natural comeback would have been an inquiry regarding the nature of this concern, but McKenzie didn't make it. Instead he went back to studying his slip of paper.

It was just as well, as I couldn't have expanded very much on that particular point. The monk in question, whose name was Dennis Feeney, had conveyed a sense of urgency but skimped on details, saying only that it was "a matter of life and death" and that I was Swickard's "only hope."

Those purple phrases had been intended to entice me, coming, as they did, straight from the kind of fiction Brother Dennis knew I read compulsively. Detective fiction. When I'd dropped out of the seminary over questions that couldn't be answered there, I'd escaped for a time into my favorite kind of stories. Mystery stories. And in those stories I'd found a new plan for my life. I'd decided that I'd answer my daunting, unanswered questions the way my heroes solved their cases, by hitting the streets and looking for clues. By seeking out every mystery, no matter how small, in the hope that even the smallest would contain clues to the biggest. And I'd kept at it, on and off, for two decades.

So Brother Dennis had had good reason to believe I'd drop everything and cross an ocean for his "matter of life and death." But he'd been wrong. Unknown to him, I'd sworn off my addiction to real life mysteries, though I still found a safe haven in fictional ones. I'd quit the real mean streets because one of my cases had caused a death and I hadn't been able to get over that.

Over the course of several tense phone calls, I'd convinced the monk that I wasn't going to go. The always scatterbrained but normally affable man had grown angry with me, had declared that he'd go to Africa himself, despite his age and failing health, and to hell with me.

That very night I'd found guidance in a detective novel, one I'd opened at random, like a believer who opens his Bible randomly, looking for a nudge from God. The story had been about a detective so heartbroken over a dead love that he'd accepted an assignment in a distant, exotic locale simply because it would offer him a chance to disappear, to take his own life in a place where no one would notice and no one would care. And I'd known immediately that I would do the same thing. I'd go to a far-off, exotic place, not to kill myself—I'd have done that months before if I'd been able—but to disappear. I'd stick my neck out one last time, and so far out that some helpful party would be unable to resist the temptation to chop at it. I had called Brother Dennis back even before I'd closed the sacred book and told him I'd changed my mind.

I examined McKenzie's office. As I'd done in my hotel and the friendly adjoining bar, and had attempted with less success to do with Nairobi as a whole, I concentrated on the familiar, trying to tie myself in to this strange new context. The director's worn pseudo-Swedish furniture could have been found in the offices of any number of ne'er-do-well charities in the States. And the striped wallpaper was so familiar I convinced myself that I remembered it from the break room of a newspaper where I'd once worked.

My little game broke down at that point. The classroom-size and very functional florescent light fixtures were only slightly out of place, but the garish acoustical tiles above them, alternately gold and red and blue, were as unfamiliar as McKenzie's soft burr, which was more pronounced now as he reclaimed my attention.

"So you dropped everything and came over here. You and Philip must have been very close."

Wrong again, I thought, and smiled. The fact that McKenzie hadn't questioned me about my secondhand concerns for Swickard suggested that he understood them better than I did, perhaps even shared them. I wondered if I could squeeze him for information without revealing my own ignorance. Then again, why did I care if I looked ridiculous to this stranger? I was going to look ridiculous to everyone in Kenya, and the sooner I got down to it the better.

"I wouldn't say we were close. I helped him out with a

problem once." I'd explained away a bag of marijuana that had turned up in Swickard's car, but mentioning that to the director would have led to an endless digression. "I'd like to help him now if he needs help. Are you aware of any problems at the mission?"

"No," McKenzie said a trifle quickly. "Just the ongoing problems of too many needy souls and not enough money." That pat answer required so little of his attention that his eyes were free to stray from mine to the wall facing the noisy windows. On it hung a portrait of a moon-faced unsmiling man. I'd seen his impassive visage at the airport and every place I'd visited since, even the bars. It was the president of Kenya.

"Yesterday I saw something a mile or so from here that I didn't quite understand," I said. "Policemen raiding a church."

It wasn't news to the mission director. "You've seen the posters for the election surely. There's naturally some tension leading up to it. Our churches, some of them, have become centers for the dissatisfaction with the current government. There have been incidents." Again his eyes flickered to the portrait on the wall. "Incidents regretted by all parties, I'm sure."

By some more than others, I was sure. I'd gotten the same guarded answer from everyone I'd questioned regarding the police raid. I saw no point in scaring McKenzie or in dragging out our interview.

"If you could suggest the best way to reach the mission," I said, getting to the point of my visit at last, "I'd be most grateful. Is there train or bus service, or should I try to rent a car?"

To my surprise, the delicate man before me wasn't through with the delicate subject. "Speaking out on behalf of the people, you know, is a fine thing. On behalf of free elections and democratic reforms. But being around for the people after the elections, continuing our work, is important, too."

I noted that he'd verbally allied his society with the dissident churches but didn't comment on it.

"As it happens, we're very close to an agreement with the government. A rapprochement. They have asked the country's religious leaders to act as observers of the coming elections. To work with the government to insure fairness. Most have agreed."

"Including your society?"

"We're not particularly hierarchical, Mr. Keane. I function as a support for the missionaries in the field. I can't speak in their names or give them orders, even when those orders would be in their best interests. I can only advise. I have advised."

Things were beginning to come together. "Philip Swickard is a critic of the government?"

"He has spoken out about some problems in his area, yes. Which is why I was curious about your relationship with Philip. Your visit could be a godsend for us. I mean, you and I could be in a position to help one another. I could arrange transportation for you to the mission. And you could talk to Philip, discuss. . ."

"Rapprochement?"

McKenzie almost winked. "Tell him what you saw yesterday at that church. Ask him to moderate his tone in exchange for the government's promise of fairness in the elections. Ask him to remember that the Crown Hill Society is here for the long term."

I saw no harm in that, especially if it meant I wouldn't have to drive to the mission alone. As it turned out, I wouldn't be driving at all.

I told McKenzie he had a deal, and he flashed me his

exploded-piano smile. "Splendid. As it happens, we have a plane flying out there tomorrow. Just a little one, you know, but I'm sure you won't mind that. Have you been taking your malaria medicine?"

"For ten days, almost."

"Two weeks would be better, but there's no help for that. How are your languages?"

"My English is okay. My Latin is a little rusty."

Through a grimace, McKenzie said, "Perhaps Father Swickard can remedy that. The local language in the Somolet area is Nihuru, but many of the people you'll meet will speak English. Almost all of them will speak Swahili to one degree or another. It's the language that allows the various tribes to communicate with one another. A few words of Swahili will help you make a good impression. *Jambo* is hello, *kwaheri* good-bye. *Tafadhali* is please, and *asante* thank you. *Asante sana* is thank you very much."

"*Asante sana*," I said for practice.

"How about your kit? It's rugged country out there. It pays to dress for it."

"I didn't pack much."

"I see. But you're well fixed for money, I suppose, as you're staying at the New Stanley."

I was well fixed for money, for once. Brother Dennis, who was a very successful artist in addition to being a monk, was bankrolling the expedition. I conveyed this with a nod.

"Good. I'll give you the name and address of a chap near here." He began scribbling on the back of the telephone message slip he still held. "Perfectly reliable. Tell him where you're going, and he'll set you up with everything you need. I'll call with particulars on the flight."

We shook on it, and I started for the office door.

"Be sure to get a good hat," McKenzie called after me.

"You're on the equator, you know, or as near to it as makes no never mind. It's best to be wary of the sun out there. It's best to be wary in general."

# CHAPTER TWO

So far I'd received more than my share of vague and threatening advice. Go quietly, from the old woman in the street. And McKenzie's contribution: Be wary.

Shapar Salhab, the outfitter to whom McKenzie directed me, gave me only very specific advice, though not all of it was comforting. Wear light colors, light fabrics, long pants and shirts with long sleeves that could be rolled up and down as the conditions required. Get a good pair of walking shoes or lightweight boots, the boots preferable because they offered some protection against snake bite, which was the disquieting part of Salhab's spiel.

His shop was large but narrow, with shelves on each side wall running up to a dim ceiling. The assistants worked with long poles equipped with clamps to reach goods on the topmost shelves. On one wall the pattern of shelving was broken by a little booth set almost against the ceiling. In it sat a white-haired man who eyed me gravely.

He seemed to be silently asking me the question I was asking myself: Why bother with new clothes if your plan is to disappear? I silently replied with the same excuse I'd used the day before, when I'd avoided the crime-ridden Uhuru Park. There was no need to rush things. The place with the greatest potential for me appeared to be Swickard's mission. I might as well show up there properly equipped, so as not to arouse the priest's suspicions. And looking like every other tourist, so I'd attract no special notice, so the memory of me

21

would fade all the more quickly.

Shapar Salhab was an Indian gentleman who followed his own advice regarding fabrics to the extent of dressing entirely in wrinkled white cotton. He saw me in khaki and lots of it. The only exceptions were olive green boots whose uppers were woven of some man-made material resistant to fangs, as Salhab demonstrated with repeated jabs of his long nails.

Like McKenzie, the Indian stressed the importance of a hat. He actually urged me toward a modern version of a pith helmet, but my willingness to look ridiculous for the locals had its limits. With that in mind, I also rejected a broad-brimmed safari number and an Australian-looking thing. It had one side of its brim pinned to the crown and a leather chin strap long enough to double as a sling in the event of a broken arm.

I settled on a hat that, while made of canvas and approximately the color of my new boots, was the size and shape of the one Humphrey Bogart had worn to play Sam Spade.

The sales slips for it and all my other purchases were placed by Salhab in a little wire basket, along with my banknotes. He then hoisted the basket to the ceiling by yanking vigorously on a closed circuit of string. As soon as the basket had gotten as high as it would go, some unseen mechanism fired it across the room on a wire tramway. It disappeared into the little booth set in the wall, the one containing the white-haired man, identified now as Salhab's father and the store's cashier.

My change and receipts returned via the same curious route. After I'd thanked Salhab, I looked up to the booth and received an encouraging nod from the old man, who raised one thin palm in a benediction that was more reassuring somehow than my sun hat and snake-proof boots.

\* \* \*

I arrived at the airport early the next morning in compliance with McKenzie's telephoned instructions. It wasn't the airport I'd used to reach Nairobi, Jomo Kenyatta International Airport, with its small-town terminal but big reassuring runways. This was a tiny operation, an airstrip really, located a long cab ride west of the city. I'd been told to ask for the Great Rift Flying Service, a name that had sounded solid and reassuring over the phone, but inspired less confidence when seen on a hand-painted sign atop a little hut.

The single-engine plane on the runway side of that hut had been professionally painted—white with red stripes—but that had been some decades ago. It sat with its rounded tail in the grass, the recently risen sun giving its Plexiglas an orange glow.

A man in shorts and a T-shirt balanced on a ladder, holding a fuel hose to an opening in the high wing. "Good morning," he called to me. "Beautiful morning to fly. You're Mr. Keane then, are you? Excellent. I'm Noah and this is my ark. Beauty, isn't she? A Cessna, from your country. A lot of people call any little plane a Cessna, but this is the real thing."

I experienced a shot of déjà vu, a not unwelcome thing on this strange continent. "Someone told me that about a Piper Cub once," I said.

"Pipers, Cessnas," Noah said equitably. "Pretty much birds of a feather, you know. They have their champions, their partisans, in the flying community who think they're worlds apart. To non-flyers they're much of a muchness. Like the Irish and the Brits, you know. They see differences worth fighting over. To the rest of the world, they're peas in a pod. "So you flew in a Cub, did you? I've always wanted to try one. Did you like it?"

"Everything but the landing," I said. I'd ended up kissing the instrument panel, but I didn't mention that to Noah. It would definitely have invited additional questions and might have been bad luck.

"You'll like my landings, I promise you. Those big balloon tires make it child's play. Could land you on a corrugated steel roof and get a compliment."

He climbed down from his ladder then, rewound the hose, and shook my hand. I noticed that his blue ball cap bore a gothic D.

"You're a fan of the Tigers?" I asked, ready to trade Al Kaline stories.

"Nope. Of *Magnum P.I.*, that American television show. We had it on one of the stations a few years back. Couldn't get my fill of it. Hawaii and all. Lady doctor I was flying around back then used to tease me terribly. When she got home to America, she sent me this cap. Just like Magnum's, you know? Though I guess I'd be T.C. more likely, that black chap with the helicopter who always saves Magnum's bacon."

In speech, Noah was closer to Higgins, the show's irascible majordomo. As he finished loading the plane, he told me he'd attended a university with an eye toward a career in medicine. Then he'd fallen in love with flying and that had been that.

My new canvas duffel bag went in last. I'd left my borrowed Samsonite in the care of the New Stanley with instructions to return it c.o.d. to its rightful owner, a New York lawyer, when I failed to return.

The inside of the plane was small but not cramped and smelled of gasoline, though that might have been Noah, who climbed in next to me still wiping his hands. I was comforted by his presence at my left side. The Piper Cub of infamous memory had tandem seating, with the pilot tucked away in back where it was impossible to keep an eye on him.

I watched carefully now as Noah went through a checklist

and started the engine. The instruments on the black panel danced to life while the propeller drove a welcome blast of cool air through the open windows of the cabin.

Noah alternately tapped and adjusted the instruments. I sat reading a series of advisory placards stuck between the round dials, starting with the one closest to the pilot: "Never exceed 170 m.p.h." "Intentional spins prohibited," the one between us advised. The one on the panel directly in front of me read, "Occupancy by more than two elephants not recommended."

Noah was smiling apologetically. "Bush pilot humor," he shouted.

On the Cub flight, the pilot and I had worn headsets and chatted conversationally via an intercom. Noah offered me only a pair of foam earplugs. I had them firmly in place by the time he'd taxied to the end of the grass runway and checked the engine and controls.

"Close your window," he shouted, showing me how by slamming his.

We were rolling before I'd gotten the hinged panel on my side fastened and in the air only seconds later. Noah spoke into a hand mike as he banked us away from the rising sun, but I couldn't make out the words. He might have been talking to air traffic control or saying good-bye to his girlfriend.

We'd left the outermost suburbs of Nairobi behind us by the time we'd climbed to our very modest cruising altitude. Only three thousand feet according to the clock hands of the altimeter. Barely high enough, it seemed to me, to clear the gray green hills before us. Far to the north were cone-shaped mountains we wouldn't have cleared and a shimmering that must have been a large lake.

Noah was shouting information about our flight that he could have whispered back on the ground when he'd been discussing his tastes in television shows. "The trip's three hundred miles, almost on the nose. We've a wind behind us today, so we'll make it in a little over two hours. Relax and enjoy it."

His voice jumped an octave on those closing instructions, and I realized I was sitting so rigidly that I'd yet to make use of my seat back. I loosened my grip on my knees and unlocked my spine. We'd already topped the highest of the hills, which helped my breathing. Before us lay a rolling plain, gray green like the hills at first but warming to a tawny brown as the sun continued to rise at our backs. There were small houses, farms, and trees in some number, adding a brighter green to the landscape, but they thinned as we approached what appeared to be a sharply defined drop-off. Beyond it a sea of brown stretched to a hazy horizon.

When we reached this dividing line, Noah shouted again. "The eastern edge of the Great Rift Valley."

The ground dropped away below us, creating the illusion that we'd jumped up another thousand feet. Noah pulled back slightly on a doorknob-shaped throttle and pushed forward on the control wheel. We began to give the free altitude back.

I thought we'd level off when we reached our previous height above the ground, but we passed through it without a check, Noah shouting, "Nothing to hit until the next escarpment. That's an hour away."

By the time he'd pulled out of our shallow dive, I was convinced I could see individual blades of grass in the undulating plain beneath us. But when my guide pointed out a herd of grazing zebras, the animals were still happily toylike.

We paralleled a dirt track for a time, once passing a heavily loaded truck whose speed across the ground almost reconciled me to air travel. I was feeling good enough about it to actually wave as we overflew an airstrip where a single plane was being unloaded. Then Noah rocked his wings aggressively to his pals on the ground, and I was gripping my knees again.

Not long afterward he pointed to the south, to a dark patch of ground, a mile or more across, that looked like the shadow of a gigantic cloud moving slowly across the earth. Only there was no corresponding cloud.

"Wildebeest," Noah roared, banking the plane. "Didn't expect to see so many so far north. Your lucky day. Let's take a look."

When we reached the edge of the herd, marked by a wavering fringe of red dust, Noah pulled the throttle back until the engine was idling. "Mustn't scare the little beauties," he said in an almost normal voice.

We glided down across the moving body. I fixated on the tightly packed, shifting mass like a sailor hypnotized by approaching rocks. The nautical analogy was apt in other ways. The always changing yet constant surface of narrow backs below me reminded me of the ocean, whose countless moving crests made up a complex whole. There was even a glint of sun off wavelets, though in this case the wavelets were curved black horns raised here and there above the surging mass.

We sailed on and on across that dark churning, the shadow of the plane sidling closer and closer as we descended. It was very close when I sighted gaps in the herd and then its ragged edge.

"That was fun," Noah said and pushed in the throttle. The engine became a presence again. We gathered speed but didn't immediately climb. I caught sight of a straggler's black eye, very close and turned upward in fear.

"You and me both," I said.

## CHAPTER THREE

The rest of the flight was uneventful, or seemed so after our strafing of the wildebeests. We sighted a line of high ground perpendicular to our course that Noah called a "false escarpment." He turned north to parallel it until we came to a cut made by a broad brown river. We followed the river west, Noah pointing out every sunbathing crocodile as though each new one was the first. Once, unaided, I spotted a hippo, whose fat back looked like a sandbar in the brown water.

Our destination airfield snuck up on me. Noah was pointing out an emerald green field of tea to my right when his voice suddenly became clearly audible. I realized that he'd pulled back the throttle again. I looked over the nose and saw a strip of packed earth with an orange windsock on a pole at one end. Then we were flashing over a parked jeep and a waving man.

Noah banked around, said, "Brace for impact," and set the balloon tires down so lightly I heard more than felt our arrival.

Grinning, he taxied us close to the parked jeep before shutting the engine down. He had a checklist for this, the flip side of the one he'd used to start the engine. While he read it through, I studied the man in the jeep, wondering if he'd been sent to take me to Philip Swickard or, if not, whether I'd be able to talk him into a ride. Only when the propeller had come to a stop did I consider a third possibility: that the man might be the priest himself.

I'd not seen Swickard since my seminary days, almost a quarter century gone, and I hadn't studied him closely then, so my mental picture was hazy. I remembered an attitude more than a face, a haughty formality unusual in a graduate student, even one studying for the priesthood. The hauteur might have been a compensation for Swickard's other trademark: his lack of size. He wasn't much above five feet tall, certainly nothing like five and a half, and thin, when I'd known him, to boot.

The man in the jeep was obscured by its dusty windshield. What I mostly saw was straw hat. But when he climbed down, it really was down, and I knew he was the little priest I'd come so far to see.

I climbed down myself, stiffly and awkwardly, and he was there with his hand out and an odd smile on his face, a smile that was half pucker. "McKenzie got a call through to let me know you were coming, but not until after you'd left. Owen Keane. If he'd said Michael Crosley was coming to see me, I wouldn't have been more surprised."

That was saying something. Crosley, another member of our seminary class, had passed the last twenty-four years in his grave. Those twenty plus years might have been forty for the damage they'd done to Swickard. His thin sandy hair, which would have covered his ears if it hadn't been stuck back behind them, had gone silvery. His brow was as creased as mine, and the scalp revealed by his pushed-back hat had the pink and spotted look of skin too fair to tan no matter how much sun it got. His blue eyes were faded and deep set, which made their lack of color seem like an inner light, an illusion enhanced by deep lines radiating from their corners like a permanently etched corona. Only his thin mouth maintained its old primness, which was especially apparent now that his initial smile had faded. His attire, short-sleeved white shirt and dark trousers, might have been prim, too, if not for the light coating of red dust he wore.

The priest had been conducting his own examination. "You're gray enough," he said at length. "Otherwise, you don't seem to have changed. How can that be?"

Before I could thank him for the compliment, he yanked it away. "Congenital immaturity must be the fountain of youth."

Noah demanded his attention then. There were supplies to be unloaded, checked, and transferred to the jeep. The last step was signing for them, but Swickard hesitated over that, looking from the paperwork to me as though I were a suspect item on the manifest. The sensitive pilot went off to check the oil in the Cessna.

"Why are you here, Owen?" Swickard asked when we were as alone as we were going to get.

I thought it was a question better discussed in a shadier spot, perhaps over a cool drink. Then it came to me that Swickard wanted his answer before he signed for the supplies, before Noah was gone and he was stuck with me. The meaning of his opening remark — about McKenzie waiting to call until after I'd taken off — had been perfectly plain. The priest would have refused permission for my visit if he'd been asked in advance. I decided that, whatever Swickard's life and death problem was, it wasn't loneliness.

"Brother Dennis sent me," I said. "He said he'd been corresponding with you and that you were in some kind of trouble. He thought I might be able to help."

That was every card I had, laid out on the table. There was no time for anything but bare honesty, but that wasn't the only reason I tried it. I was reacting to Swickard and his pruney smile the same way I'd reacted to them back in the seminary, matching the obvious chip on his shoulder with one of my own. Even though I needed his help more than he appeared to need mine.

In the end he signed, shaking his head all the while. Noah shook my hand, passed me my new hat, which I'd left on the backseat of the plane, and was off.

Swickard watched the departing Cessna for a long time. Then he said, "You'll have to forgive my lack of hospitality, Owen. Put it down to disorientation. I mentioned you in my last letter to Dennis—just mentioned you, didn't extend an invitation—and now here you are, like a conjured spirit."

"You didn't ask Dennis to send me?"

"Certainly not."

"But you told him you were in some kind of trouble."

"No more than usual." He was still watching the sky, though the plane had disappeared. I noted that he stood slightly stooped, giving up an inch or two of height he couldn't really spare, and that the brim of his farmer's hat had been broken in several places and expertly rewoven.

"No real trouble," he said, moving slowly toward the jeep. "No, I mentioned you in that letter because of an odd coincidence. You happened to be on my mind. And then a couple of events occurred that would have reminded me of you if I hadn't already been thinking of you, things that reminded me of that old blowup back at St. Aelred's. The one that ended with your being kicked out."

The way I remembered it, I'd left the seminary of my own free will, but I didn't argue. Swickard hadn't paused for argument.

"You were trying to trace Michael Crosley, as I recall. We all thought he'd dropped out of school and run away. And you somehow got looking for an old manuscript you thought might be valuable."

"A sonnet," I said. "I remember."

To Swickard it all seemed to be as ancient as *The Odys-*

*sey* and about as likely. He'd made it as far as the driver's seat of the jeep, but he was seated facing out the side, his sandaled feet hanging down like a child's. His eyes seemed even deeper set, as though they were sinking into his head as he gazed backward in time.

"What happened around here to remind you of that?" I asked.

The blue eyes blinked and focused on me. "Just a couple of coincidences, as I said. Parallels. A young man's run away. My assistant, actually, Daniel. He's about Crosley's age. The age we all were when Crosley. . ."

"What about the poem? What's the parallel to that?"

"Something's gone missing. An artifact, not a poem. The resemblance is that this thing is old and valuable—oddly valuable, all of a sudden. It's a sword. An ugly curved thing that once belonged to one of the old-time chiefs, name of Wauki. The Sword of Wauki."

# CHAPTER FOUR

On the drive to the mission the only further information I could get from the priest was that the two mysterious occurrences had happened a few days apart. First — almost a month ago now — the assistant, Daniel, had run off. A few days later the sword had been stolen. Swickard wouldn't speculate on whether the two events were connected, wouldn't tell me who Wauki was or why his sword was suddenly valuable. He wouldn't do anything but focus on his driving.

I couldn't blame him for that. The road was dirt and badly rutted, the ruts rock-hard remnants of some rainier time. This track ran along the river Noah had followed, but not at water level. The road edged a series of bluffs overlooking the muddy stream, bluffs with no guardrails, which made Swickard's single-mindedness even easier to forgive.

Eventually we turned north away from the river. The mission was a quarter mile from the naked bluffs in a nice stand of trees, a couple of which supported an overloaded clothesline. Some of the clothes were women's. Swickard didn't speak to that point, only casually identifying the trees as acacias. There were two main buildings, a house and a church, the house the bigger and the more impressive of the two by far.

The priest explained the disparity as we climbed down from the jeep. "Welcome to Crown Hill Somolet, as we're officially designated. The locals call the place Crucifixion, after the church. On bad days, I call it that myself. This imposing pile is the former 'great house' of a big farm or estate that was broken into smaller holdings back in the sixties. The church was built around that time, but they couldn't begin to match the materials used in the house. The man who built the estate — in the thirties I'm told — was an eccentric English lord."

The eccentric lord's house was made of square-cut brown stone and had a roof of reddish brown tile. The front porch, spanning the full width of the house and backed by walk-out windows, was columned and deep and very inviting after the short ride in the topless jeep. The Lord's house, in contrast, was a simple frame structure with a roof of the corrugated steel that Noah had bragged he could land on. Atop the roof, a simple frame supported a single bell. Around the church and the house and a few outbuildings ran a chest-high stone wall that gave the place the feeling of a compound.

"Keeps the bigger animals out," Swickard said of the wall. "The bigger, clumsier animals."

He took me to make a visit to the Church of the Crucifixion. It was as plain inside as out and might have belonged to any Christian denomination, save for the large crucifix that hung behind the altar table. It was a rudely carved and very striking piece, the figure's whole form so contorted with pain that the cross itself was bent with it.

"The work of a local craftsman whose name has been lost," said the priest, who had been watching me closely. "Belongs in the Vatican art collection or at least in the cathedral in Nairobi. But I'd miss it sorely. Anyone who doubts the power of iconography should try saying Mass with Him at his back. Let's just say that you're never allowed to lose yourself in mindless repetition."

Later we sat on the broad verandah with the cool drinks I'd imagined earlier in our hands. They were only lemonade, which was disappointing but somehow symbolic of the house tour, a walk through a large, stone-floored space that was clean and cool but surprisingly empty. Swickard's living quarters were simple and spare. The remainder of the rooms were dedicated to classes not in session and ministries temporarily shut down. The only people I'd met were the rectory's housekeeper, Etta, and its cook, Ruth, both older women and the owners of the bloomers I'd seen drying on the line. Five children of varying ages—orphans Swickard had taken in—were at play in the backyard. They and the women slept in the largest of the outbuildings, a stone barracks that must have housed the farmhands back in the English lord's day.

"You've come at a slow time for us," my host said, his sharp nose sniffing at his lemonade as though it were a rare vintage. "This is farming country. Our students and teachers and other workers are always on call. Parish work takes second place at planting time and harvesting time."

Then he watched me for so long I finally realized that he expected me to question that plausible explanation. "Is that so?" I asked to oblige him.

"Not really. I mean, it's true most years. But this year is different. My poor rapport with the government over the upcoming elections has scared some people away. But that's not the whole story either. My influence with my parishioners is being undercut, undermined."

"By the government?"

"No," the priest said. "By a mystic and by a ghost." His voice still had a Midwestern flatness that gave his odd pronouncement an anchorman's authority.

Before I could ask for an explanation, he suddenly went on the offensive. "Speaking of ghosts, I've been racking my brain for the reason Dennis might have sent you, a ghost from my past, all the way out here to Somolet, a place even

35

most Kenyans have never heard of."

More lemonade sniffing. "And?" I prompted.

"I've remembered that in one of his recent letters he said he was worried about you. He said you were very depressed over the suicide of a young woman, that you blamed yourself for it, that it had happened as a result of one of your, ah, investigations. According to Dennis, you've spent the past two years in a kind of funk or malaise. He wasn't sure you'd ever come out of it."

I wasn't planning to. "What does that have to do with your troubles?"

"Don't you see?" Swickard asked, leaning forward in his rattan chair. "Maybe Dennis made up all that about me needing help, or at least blew something I'd written him about my assistant running off and a sword being stolen all out of proportion. Maybe he did it just to get you off your duff. Maybe he thought coming over here would do you good, make you feel less sorry for yourself. I know I've always found it impossible to sustain self-pity in a country where the people have so little and face so much."

It was an ironic possibility: Brother Dennis and I might each have seen the Africa trip as a cure for my heartsickness. The difference being that I didn't expect to survive the treatment. But Swickard was jumping to yet another thought.

"Or maybe I'm the cure. Maybe Dennis sees me as your confessor, the man who can finally get you to decide what you believe in, if in fact you believe in anything. He's concerned, you see, that you've come so far in your life without declaring for one side or the other, for belief or non-belief. Incidentally, that's what I meant by the crack I made back at the airstrip about your congenital immaturity. I think it was Andrew Greeley who called the inability to decide once and for all about one's belief in God to be the epitome of immaturity.

"I was quite surprised that you didn't take offense at that. The Owen Keane I remember would have come right back at me. You just ignored it."

"Must be that pesky malaise," I said. "Mind if we go back to the government and the elections for a moment? Or would you rather explain that comment you just made about the ghost and the mystic undermining you?"

I was remembering more and more about Philip Swickard. For instance, he was a person who used a laugh to express disdain as often as amusement. He laughed that way now and said, "I'll have to explain my relationship with the government first. It's the background or context for everything else. But it's complicated."

"Director McKenzie told me you've spoken out against the government. In fact, he asked me to try to get you to lay off. But he didn't say what you were criticizing them for."

"Probably because the subject matter changes so regularly. The form of the corruption keeps changing; the government never changes. The latest outrage involves land grabbing, something out of an old Hollywood western."

He made a sweeping gesture toward the rolling land beyond the compound wall. "Once this was all a great estate. I mean, originally it was unimproved country, the territory of the native tribe. Then the crazy Englishman I mentioned got title to a thousand acres of it somehow and created his great farm. Large holdings like that were the rule in colonial Kenya. Then, when independence came, this estate and others like it were broken up into a number of small farms—they call them *shambas*—and turned over to the native people. That was land reform.

"Now, in the Great Rift Valley and little tributary valleys like this one, that reform is being reversed. Powerful men are taking small holdings from the families who have been working them for decades and giving them to their own supporters. Or worse, they're often just keeping the little farms, consolidating them into great private estates. In some cases, whole villages have been displaced.

"It would be bad enough if the farmers were being bought out. But that's not the case. They're being driven off their land by the threat of violence and by violence itself. Corrupt officials are promoting antagonisms among tribes that have lived together in peace for decades, so they can rob all parties involved. It started up north, but it's been moving this way, sweeping toward this little valley like a plague of locusts.

"That's the situation the government is pressuring McKenzie to pressure you to pressure me to ignore. And the joke is, none of you need to have bothered. At this critical moment, right before these important elections, my influence with the people has been compromised by two men who have nothing to do with the government."

"The mystic and the ghost," I said.

The children who had been playing in the backyard came around the corner of the house at a run, saw us, and scattered. The single exception was a boy of about ten, stick thin except for a prominent belly and dressed only in ragged brown shorts and low-topped canvas shoes the color of the dust, each shoe worn through at the toe.

"There's my good friend Basil," Swickard said. "He came to us on the feast day of St. Basil the Great. He's a boy after your own heart, Owen. A great noticer of things.

"Basil, come here and meet Owen, from America. He and I went to school together. Owen is a good man."

Basil came forward a step or two, stopping abruptly when I made the mistake of saying hello.

"Run along now," Swickard said, and the boy trotted off.

"What were we saying?"

"You were about to tell me a ghost story."

"Yes, of course. Ghost was a poor choice of words. He's just a man, a stranger who's come forward to claim the leadership of the local tribe, the Nihuru, and, in his spare time, to whittle away at my authority. He claims to be the reincarnation of Wauki, a chief killed by the British a hundred years ago."

"The original owner of the missing sword?"

"The same. This man, a stranger, as I said, to everyone around here, just appeared one day five or six weeks ago and calmly announced that he was old Wauki, back from the grave. He's been a problem for Chief Joseph Wamba, the legitimate leader of the Nihuru, from the start. And this new Wauki is no great fan of the Church or me.

"Then there's this business of the sword. Before he'd been here a week, this Wauki was demanding the return of his sword. It was in the private collection of a retired schoolteacher who lives about a half a mile down that road, Elizabeth Chesney. She refused him, of course, and he gave her a cycle of the moon in which to change her mind. The sword disappeared shortly afterward. Now the deadline is looming and poor Elizabeth has nothing to turn over."

"What's the mystic's connection to this?"

"He hasn't one, so far as I know. Wauki is bothering the community in general. Mugo the mystic is my own private thorn. He's a Gandhian figure, which I mean literally. Wears his head shaved and dresses in white robes. Has a camp somewhere southwest of here in the old forest.

"What Wauki has done to my temporal authority, Mugo is doing to my spiritual authority. He shows up everywhere around the parish, gently questioning my teachings, stirring up the old beliefs.

"Not that he's the least bit underhanded. He actually came here to see me not long ago. Perhaps a month. No, just over a month. Daniel was still here, I remember. Mugo sat where you're sitting now. I found him to be quite charming, quite the smiling rascal. And well educated, though he wouldn't say where he'd come by his education."

Swickard stopped abruptly, considered his glass, considered me. He was trying to decide whether to tell me something. I tried not to look as tired as I felt.

After a full minute, he asked, "Do you remember my saying back at the airstrip that I was thinking about you even before Daniel ran off and the sword was stolen?"

I nodded.

"It surprised me that you didn't pounce on that. The old Owen Keane would have."

He waited for me to pounce on it now, so I gave it a try. "Brother Dennis mentioned me in one of his letters, mentioned his concern for me," I said. "That would have had me in your mind."

Swickard was shaking his head before I'd finished. "That was part of it, of course. But Dennis has mentioned you so often over the years that I don't really take special notice of it anymore. No, the man who really got me thinking about you was this mystic, Mugo.

"He mentioned you during our talk. I don't mean he used your name. It was something he was trying to tell me about a certain kind of person. A fixated person, though he didn't use the word 'fixated.' He called him 'the hunter who doesn't believe in his prey.' Got that?"

I nodded again, but he repeated it anyway.

"'The hunter who doesn't believe in his prey.' Not 'the hunter of imaginary prey,' since that could imply belief, however misplaced, on the part of the hunter. And not 'the hunter who doesn't expect to find his prey.' Not simple disillusionment or discouragement, in other words.

"If I understood him correctly, he was talking about a person who continues to hunt — is compelled to hunt — something he can't bring himself to believe in. When I heard that, I thought of you."

He peered down into his nearly empty glass as though the bits of lemon floating there were tea leaves. "I thought of you and here you are. Tell me how this Kenyan mystic could have foretold your coming. You can't; it's too bizarre. Like Dennis sending you across an ocean on a whim. Owen Keane here in Somolet. What could top that, I wonder?"

Owen Keane nowhere, I thought, and raised my glass to it.

## CHAPTER FIVE

The priest and I concluded that first talk by discussing the length of my visit. Noah's next scheduled appearance was a month away, and Swickard didn't want me underfoot that long, no matter what Brother Dennis's hopes for my spiritual revival might be. He proposed that we give it a week. At the end of that time, barring some breakthrough on my part, he'd call Nairobi—if that happened to be the day the phones were working—and order a plane. He was confident that I'd be more than happy to pay for one by then.

In the meantime, he had work to do. He suggested that I remain inside the compound, suggested it casually, his tone conveying the certainty that I had nowhere else to go.

But as it happened, I already had a little excursion in mind. When the priest was out of sight inside the house, I made my way through the front gate of the compound and onto the dusty road. Elizabeth Chesney, the woman who'd lost the suddenly valuable sword, lived half a mile down that road, according to the priest. There was plenty of time to visit her and get back before dinner.

In setting out to make that visit, I was ignoring more than Swickard's advice. I was also ignoring—consciously ignoring—his idea that Brother Dennis had sent me all this way for my own welfare, not the priest's. I needed there to be a problem, a mystery, a source of danger. Otherwise I was wasting my time. So I was sticking to the premise that I was in Africa because an old classmate was in trouble, whether he knew it or not, period. And of the troubles I'd heard about so far, the most interesting one involved Wauki and his stolen sword.

I'd only gotten a hundred yards or so down the dirt road when I was stopped by a small voice calling, "Hi!" It was Basil, running after me, carrying the hat I'd left on the front porch of the mission.

I thanked him for it, but he didn't nod in acknowledgment until my head was properly covered. He didn't smile even then, but he seemed content, if not quite sure of me. His light brows were arched and the large eyes beneath them narrowed in a look of steady examination bordering on fascination. I returned the compliment. His hair, which featured a slight but definite widow's peak, was very short, which made his ears, standing straight out from the sides of his head, prominent despite their average size. The left ear was adorned at the top with a loop of tiny red and blue beads.

"Thanks again," I said and continued down the road. Basil followed a few paces behind. After a time, I tried to make conversation, asking about the planted fields we were passing and commenting on the heat and the mosquitoes. Basil didn't have much small talk. But when I asked him if he knew the way to Chesney's, he trotted past me and took up station a few feet ahead.

It was just as well that I had a guide. Swickard's passing comment had led me to believe that Chesney's house would be right on the main road. It actually sat some distance from it, at the end of its own lane, a cottage with a heavily thatched roof and light blue siding, surrounded by a flower garden that seemed, at first glance, to be running wild. When we reached the stone path that wound through the flowers, I decided that the droning confusion was actually the gardener's intention.

By then someone was on the front steps waiting for us, a

white-haired woman in a straight blue dress a shade darker than the cottage walls. Her figure was square and solid and very erect. I guessed that she'd been alerted by the dog that stood at her side, an immense brown drooling thing with black jowls.

"Good afternoon, Basil," the woman called out in a genteel English accent. She identified herself as the owner of the cottage by adding, "Who is this you've brought me?"

She was forced to call to Basil because the boy had stopped at the entrance to the garden. "He doesn't like my bees," Chesney told me. "I don't suppose a lion would frighten him, but a bee does."

I introduced myself as a friend of Philip Swickard's. I would normally then have passed off my visit to Chesney's cottage as a social call and snuck up on the subject of the sword by and by. But now something—the old woman's trusting sun-damaged face or the presence of her drooling dog or the exploration of my naked forearm by one of her bees—made me unusually direct.

"I'd like to hear the story of your stolen sword" was how I put it.

"Would you? Come in then. I was just thinking about tea."

She looked like the kind of person who was always making tea or ordering it up. Chesney was a do-it-yourselfer, as it turned out. She deposited me in what must have been the largest room of the cottage, leaving the dog, whose name was Reggie, to keep me company. He lost interest immediately and stretched out on a stone hearth. That left me free to look around.

The room was an odd combination of fussy parlor and armory. The white walls of the otherwise conventional room were decorated with spears and shields and clubs, the wood of which was dark with age. There was one sword, a long glittering thing with a golden hilt, mounted on the wall at an angle. The angle and a slight discoloration of the white wall suggested that there had once been two swords, crossed. I investigated, drawing only a raised head from Reggie, and found tiny white-painted brackets that must once have supported the Sword of Wauki.

Chesney entered then, the timing so perfect that she might have been watching my examination of the room, perhaps through a peephole cut in the eye of the moustached military man whose portrait overlooked Reggie's hearth.

"Yes, that's where it hung," she said, "for the past thirty years, hardly interesting anyone, crossed with that other sword, though they were a bad match.

"Sit down here, Mr. Keane, and tell me how you like your tea. Help yourself to the sandwiches, won't you?"

The sandwiches turned out to be nothing more than bread and butter, but I ate them hungrily. Swickard hadn't offered me lunch and I hadn't missed it, given the heat and the tension of the flight. Now I found I was close to ravenous.

"You must tell me something about yourself," Chesney said. "Beyond the fact that you're an American, that you've come to Kenya on very short notice, and that your visit was a complete surprise to Father Philip, I can tell very little."

She only needed a pipe and a deerstalker hat to complete the effect. My expression conveyed my admiration.

"Nothing extraordinary, I assure you," she said. "Your voice would tell anyone that you're from the eastern seaboard of the United States. But your clothes aren't American. They were purchased in Nairobi, unless I'm very much mistaken, which suggests that you didn't have much time to prepare for your visit. As to that visit being a surprise to Philip, I could say something clever about your appetite, about the suggestion that he didn't have luncheon prepared for you, but the simple truth is I know your visit was a surprise because I hadn't heard that you were coming. In a small community like ours, it would have been big news. I would have heard any number of official and unofficial reports."

She sipped her tea. "Now, to show me that there are no hard feelings, turn the tables on me. Deduce what you can of me."

I swallowed my latest helping of bread and butter and said, "You're the daughter of a soldier, John Chesney, a colonel in the British army. You never married. You're right-handed and you once taught school."

Chesney's slightly generous eyebrows had risen sharply, making furrows of the wrinkles on her forehead. Evidently she'd expected me to pass on my round of the guessing game. But she recovered quickly.

"You examined the remaining sword and saw my father's name and rank engraved on the blade. That it was my father and not some other relation, my husband say, you deduced from the age of the portrait over the fireplace, in which the sword appears and which bears the year 1937 below the artist's signature. As my last name is my father's, you concluded that I've never married. You know I am right-handed from watching me pour out the tea. But how did you know that I once taught school? I don't keep mementos of that in this room."

"Father Philip told me. I threw it in to pad my list."

She'd never stopped smiling, even when she'd been taken aback. She didn't smile any more or any less now. "Why did you come to Kenya, Mr. Keane?"

"Because Father Philip is in trouble. Or so I was told. Father Philip doesn't see it that way."

Like McKenzie the day before, Chesney didn't inquire about the nature of the trouble. Not directly. "How is the theft of the sword related to that?"

"I don't know," I said.

"And why were you the one sent to help Philip?"

She could have gotten an earful on that subject from Swickard, his whole "damaged detective seeks African cure" theory. She would surely get that earful as soon as she and the priest had their next private tea. In the meantime, there was no point in running down my reputation on what was for me a fresh continent.

"I've looked into other problems for other people in the past." Some of whom had actually welcomed the service.

Chesney still smiled her steady smile. The smile arranged the wrinkles on her face pleasantly. Even the slight bags under her eyes and their sagging lids looked jolly. "You've been very patient with my questions," she said. "So I'll be happy to tell you what I know.

"The missing sword isn't a sword at all, strictly speaking. It's a British naval cutlass of nineteenth century design. Early nineteenth century. It's the kind of weapon Horatio Nelson's men used, an ugly functional thing with a curved blade and a heavy brass guard around the hilt. It might have been left behind by one of the early naval expeditions to Mombasa out on the coast, but how it found its way into the interior and into the possession of a Nihuru chief named Wauki, no one can say.

"My father acquired it along with some other trophies from the commander of a regiment that was being transferred from East Africa to India. I'm not sure how it had ended up in that regiment's mess. It might have been a bequest of Prentice, Wauki's last foe.

"My father loved to tell the story of the sword. Unfortunately for me, I continued the tradition. So there was no shortage of people about to tell this new Wauki where his

47

trusty blade could be found. He was here asking for it within a week or two of his arrival in the area."

"And you turned him down."

"Yes, well, he didn't appear with proof of ownership, did he? Now, of course, I wish I'd given it to him. His deadline will be up with the full moon, four days from now. I don't suppose he'll believe I lost it. I'm afraid he and his followers will dig up my flower beds looking for it."

"How was the original Wauki killed? Father Philip said the British were responsible."

"Ah," Chesney said, picking up her teapot, which was a porcelain replica of her thatched-roof cottage. "Therein lies the tale, as they say." She refilled both our cups and settled back in her chair.

"The British were just arriving this far west in the last decades of the last century. They'd established a little fort on the river here, Fort Fisher, which was the name of our town until independence, when it was changed to Somolet. The British began trading with the local tribes, the Nihuru and their neighbors, and arbitrating disputes between the tribes, subtly establishing British authority.

"Late one night Wauki came to the fort, drunk as a lord. He was a big fellow, as chiefs tend to be. He accosted one of the officers, a lieutenant named Prentice, complaining about some cattle one of the other chiefs had run off. Prentice tried to throw Wauki out, laid hands on him to do it, which was a mistake. The chief drew his sword and Prentice had to grapple with him to avoid losing an ear. Or worse.

"The two of them raised such a noise that it woke every man in the fort. Before help could arrive, Prentice had got hold of the cutlass and knocked Wauki on the head with the hilt of the thing. Cracked his skull for him, though no one knew it at the time.

"The soldiers gathered the chiefs of the neighboring tribes and gave Wauki a trial, which ended with him being banished to the coast. I expect the rival chiefs were happy to be rid of him so they could raid his cattle.

"But poor Wauki never reached his Elba. He died en route from complications of a fractured skull. He was buried near Naughton Station. You flew over the spot on your way here, I expect.

"Oddly, Lieutenant Prentice is buried right next to him. Came down with fever on the way to Nairobi some years after Wauki died. They're near enough to grapple in death. Or they were before Wauki resurrected himself.

"Who knows? Perhaps Prentice has come back as well. Any memories of the playing fields of Eton you can't account for, Mr. Keane?"

"No," I said.

Chesney sighed. "Pity."

## CHAPTER SIX

Chesney drifted awhile after that, telling me stories of colonial Kenya in the order they came to her. For example, when the mantel clock struck five, it reminded her that the earliest European settlers had reset their unreliable clocks to seven each Sunday morning at dawn. Living on the equator, they knew that sunrise was never more than half an hour off true seven any day of the year.

The chiming reminded me of something altogether different. Namely that Swickard would miss me soon if I didn't get moving. I nudged Chesney back toward the topic of the missing cutlass, asking when she'd last seen it on the wall.

"It was very nearly one month ago. Not long after Wauki's demand for the sword's return. I held a little dinner party that evening, and, as you might expect, the sword was a topic of conversation because of Wauki's ultimatum. And it was there on the wall as it's always been. At least it was during the party. I've been racking my brain ever since trying to remember whether I saw the sword in its place when I locked up that night. I'm afraid I just cannot recall. I know that when I came in here the next morning it was gone."

"Was there any sign of a break-in?"

"No, but I don't suppose that anyone who really knew his business would have left a sign. My locks aren't very formidable."

"Where was Reggie during the party?"

That question pleased her, with qualifications. "You might

have said, 'I'd like to call your attention to the curious behavior of the dog that barked in the night.' And then I could have said, 'But the dog didn't bark in the night.' To which you could have replied, 'That was the curious behavior.'"

"There'd have been copyright issues," I said. "What about the dog?"

"Reggie is getting old, but he's still a good watchdog. He heard you and Basil from a long way off today, for example. However, he gets confused when the house is full of people and noise. So he might not have heard someone approach during the party. And he was shut up in my bedroom, which is on the opposite end of the house from this room and the sword, another handicap."

"Why was he shut up?"

"One of my guests, Commissioner Karari Gathitu, our local government representative, requested it. It wasn't a special or unusual request. He and Reggie have never gotten along."

"Where was Reggie after the party?"

"Asleep at the foot of my bed, as always. He never stirred, never growled, as he does when an animal is nosing about, or barked, as he will for a two-legged animal."

Which left us with the dinner party. "Aside from Mr. Gathitu, who were your guests that evening? Did Chief Wamba come?"

"No. Chief Joseph is getting on in years now and never strays very far from Agat, the village where he lives. Let me see. Father Philip was here, Dr. Rex Brocious, who runs our local clinic, Samuel Mwarai, our chief constable, and the Praeds, Norris and Lori, an Australian couple who are managing our new safari lodge. No one of whom would steal so much as a saltcellar."

And yet. Next to the sword's former place of honor on the wall was another relic, an old canvas-covered canteen, and to its left a pair of French doors, screened. With Chesney's permission, I examined them. They were locked, but the old-fashioned key resided in the old-fashioned lock, available to anyone inside the room. The screen was intact.

I unlocked the doors and stepped outside onto a patio made of the same stone as the hearth. Beyond it was the encircling flower garden. It would have been the work of a minute to have taken down the sword, opened the doors, and either handed the thing to a waiting confederate or hidden it for a later pick-up. The first alternative seemed likelier, since a return visit at a quieter time would have been noted by Reggie.

Even so, I poked around the snapdragons and petunias for a few fruitless minutes, looking for the gleam of a brass hilt. Chesney joined me there, carrying my hat, though she was bareheaded herself, her white pageboy looking thin in the full sun.

"I've had an inspiration," she said. "Why don't we recreate the party? That's what they would do in a mystery novel. You can question all the suspects at once, maybe get them contradicting one another. It will save you a great deal of time and effort."

Chesney had saved me a chunk of time already, by accepting my interest in the sword and my right to investigate its disappearance without asking for much in the way of credentials. I was so used to having my competence as a detective questioned that I stepped in now to fill the void.

"I'm not accusing your guests of anything," I said. "And I'm not a trained investigator."

She waved my hat airily. "I know. You're just a man on vacation who's distracting himself with an interesting problem. What could be more natural? And what could be more natural than my arranging a little dinner so you can meet the most prominent members of our local community? Shall we say tomorrow evening? We're very informal here, so the lack of notice won't arouse suspicion. Wauki's deadline doesn't give us time for niceties.

"We're informal as to dress as well," she assured me as she led me back through the cottage. That was a relief, since Shapar Salhab had forgotten to sell me a khaki dinner jacket.

Chesney had taken me back through the house so she could collect the last bread and butter sandwich from the tea tray. "For Basil," she said as she handed it to me.

I looked around for something to wrap it in so it would survive the walk back, saying, "He's long gone by now."

"You don't know our Basil. Shall we say cocktails at seven? I'll phone Father Philip to confirm."

As Chesney had predicted, Basil was waiting for me, just outside the realm of the bees. He took the buttered bread and waved his thanks to Chesney. By the time I'd finished my own waving, the last greasy crumb was gone.


Basil and I spoke even less on the way back than we had on the way over. The boy acted as guide again, though I could still see the outline of our outbound tracks in the dust of the road. But I was content to be led. The mental fuzziness that had plagued me in Nairobi was back in force and seemed to be pitched to the exact frequency of the buzzing insects in the little grove of trees split by our road. They were some kind of fruit trees. Mangoes perhaps.

I was so sleepy that Basil had to tell me twice to stop, once in emphatic English. When he was sure I understood, he picked up a long stick and trotted a little way up the road. There he circled something in the dust, prodding it with his stick, something that writhed in response. A snake. An iridescent green snake nearly three feet long, I saw when

Basil carried it back for my inspection.

He'd gotten its tail wound around his stick somehow. The snake's front half hung free, preceding Basil and moving left and right as he walked, like a blind man's cane. When the boy presented the snake for my inspection, I could clearly see its tongue licking my strange New Jersey scent from the air.

"Poison," Basil said.

I only had to reach out to touch the thing faster than he could pull it back, and the whole trip would be justified. But I didn't reach out. I didn't want the boy to be responsible, if only in his own mind.

"*Asante sana*," I said to him.

"You're welcome," he said to me.

Then he carried the snake to the tree it had been making for and held the stick up to a low-hanging branch. A second later, the glowing green had disappeared into the dusty leaves.

That little encounter kept me awake and alert for the rest of the walk. So alert that I made out the sound of angry chanting when we were still some way from the mission, when it was only a little louder than the buzzing in the trees. I asked Basil about it. His only reply was to quicken his step.

The sound was coming from the front of the mission compound, from a group of perhaps a dozen men gathered there. Swickard stood facing them on the top step of the porch. Even on that perch, the priest was scarcely taller than the man who fronted the chanting group. He was broad as well as tall and dressed, like me, in khaki. The crowd at his back was entirely male and dressed in every color. They fell silent as Basil and I made our way through them.

The big man in khaki turned to greet us. He had a broad, handsome face not unlike the presidential portrait I'd seen everywhere in Nairobi, although much younger. And much friendlier. He was clean shaven and his skin was so dark it had a bluish, bruised cast. The thin necklace he wore looked like it might snap at any moment or disappear into the folds of his neck. His small eyes were reduced to pupils by his smile. They fixed me with a look that had so much recognition in it I struggled to place him. Then I realized that this instant connection was just his style. His gift.

"Our visitor from America," he said in an easy baritone that went perfectly with his double-bass chest. "Welcome to the valley of the Nihuru. I am Wauki, once chief of the Nihuru. Now just Wauki."

Swickard broke in then to introduce me, irritated perhaps that Wauki was acting like he owned the place.

The big man repeated my name and bowed. "I am here to deliver a warning to the priest. I am honored to have Owen Keane as a witness to it.

"I have heard that my sword was taken from the house of Miss Chesney. I know that she is respected by everyone in the valley. So I believe that it was taken without her knowledge. I also believe that this priest is the one who took it, that it is hidden in the great house or in the church."

"In my church!" Swickard sputtered. He was mad in the way I remembered him getting mad: all swollen dignity and clenched fists.

I said, "Why would Father Swickard have any interest in your sword?"

Wauki beamed. "It is very courteous of you to call it *my* sword. Many would not. So I will tell you why the priest stole it. He has great influence with the people of my valley. He fears losing that influence to someone who will use it more wisely. More honestly."

Swickard was sputtering again. I cut him off. "How more honestly?"

"The people of the valley are being eyed hungrily by the

great lords in Nairobi. The very land beneath their feet is at risk."

"Father Swickard has spoken out about that," I said.

Wauki held up a hand as wide as my head. "He pretends to speak against it. In fact, he is the hired man of the Nairobi lords. He keeps the people, my people, quiet and complacent. He holds the head of the cow while the lords milk its very blood."

The little crowd of onlookers murmured their approval of the image. Wauki said, "Now that deception is almost over. I am giving the priest until the day I gave Miss Chesney to return my sword to me. Not one day more. If the sword is not returned to me by the full of the moon—four days hence—I will enter the mission and seize it. No man and no magic will keep me out."

It was an exit line if I ever heard one. But Wauki didn't exit. He turned to face Swickard, giving him a chance to reply. Unfortunately, the priest's dignity had now swollen to the point where it blocked speech completely.

Wauki turned back to me. And there was that look again, the look that made me feel like an open book to this stranger. A book with extra large type. "Owen Keane, have you heard my story?"

"I've heard how you died," I blurted out before I could come up with a more condolatory phrasing.

"If you heard it from a white, you heard a lie. Will you listen to the truth?"

"Always," I said.

"A good answer."

He then shocked us all by leaping onto the mission steps just below the priest, moving like a dancer, in a single light and graceful bound. He turned in the air as he leapt and so ended facing me and his followers and all but blocking

Swickard from view.

"I was here when the English came to this valley. They came first to learn of us, later to trade with us, and lastly to reign over us. I saw what they were about, but I refused to attack them. They were armed with guns, the first many of us had ever seen, and I knew my people would suffer if war came.

"But I also knew that my people would lose their land if I did nothing to help them. Then as now the arrogant lords hungered for the valley of my people. Only then the lords were white.

"One night I went alone to the fortress of the English to entreat them to spare my valley. As a token of good faith, I gave up my sword when I entered the fort. At once, the English fell upon me and bound me hand and foot.

"When my people learned of the treachery, they surrounded the fort. They were determined to save me, whatever the cost. But I knew they would be slaughtered by the English guns. I called out to them. I ordered them to go in peace and to wait in peace until I returned.

"The English carried me off, far to the east. There they murdered me, hoping to stop me from returning, as I'd promised my people I would.

"But they could not stop me, any more than this priest can stop me."

He spread his arms wide and held them there. Behind me, the onlookers began to chant again, and now I was able to make out the word they were repeating: "Wauki."

"I returned to my people before in their hour of need. Now I have returned again. I have returned to stand on the neck of any who threaten us."

His joyful smile had disappeared, and he was focused, not on the stone-faced Swickard or the chanting crowd, but on me.

## CHAPTER SEVEN

That evening the priest and I dined by the light of kerosene lamps. The main course was a meatless curry. It was very spicy, almost too spicy for me, for which Swickard apologized.

"I'm afraid my twenty years abroad have burned my tongue as well as my scalp. I often wonder how I'd take to Midwestern cooking, were I to go back. I suspect I couldn't taste it at all."

The observation would have sounded a little nostalgic and sad coming from any expatriate. Coming from Swickard, only hours after Wauki's visit, it bordered on pathetic.

He grew quiet after that, thinking, I was sure, of his lost Indiana. I asked him when he planned to return to the United States.

"I haven't made a plan. I'm not sure I ever will go back. Priests don't retire, not these days. Certainly we don't take early retirement. The closest thing I had to a plan—and it was more of a fond hope—involved my assistant Daniel. I've prayed for his priestly vocation, I can't tell you how many hours. I thought it would make the biggest difference if this mission were in the care of a priest of the people."

Swickard had forbidden any discussion of Wauki over dinner. This after he had grudgingly gone along with my idea that we search the mission for the missing sword and the only result had been a delayed meal. So I had to accept his AWOL assistant as a substitute topic.

"How long was Daniel with you?"

"Less than a year. I know what you're thinking. That I had no right to hang any serious hopes on him. That it would have taken him years of study and prayer to have made an informed decision about the priesthood.

"You're right, of course. I suppose I was grasping at straws. But Daniel showed that kind of promise, that kind of light, almost from the start. He's the nephew of Ruth, my cook, by the way. She's as upset over his disappearance as I am."

Ruth was a tall woman who habitually stood and even walked bent at the waist, perhaps in deference to her employer's stature. In addition to cooking our meal, she'd served it. She was in the room now, clearing dishes and setting out coffee cups while Swickard spoke of her as though she were miles away. I noticed that every time her nephew's name was mentioned, Ruth winced slightly, sometimes shutting her eyes with it, sometimes bowing her head.

I asked the priest if he'd gone to the police about Daniel. He laughed his mirthless laugh.

"I spoke to Chief Constable Mwarai. You'll meet him tomorrow night if Elizabeth manages to recreate her last party, as you tell me she intends to do. Mwarai is a very careful man, especially where I'm concerned. Always checks which way the political wind is blowing before he acts. Then he seldom acts at all.

"There are no political implications to Daniel's disappearance, but that hasn't kept Mwarai from not acting. He seems to think it's the most natural thing in the world for a young man with his whole life ahead of him to run far away from any contact with the priesthood."

I'd encountered an identical attitude in U.S. policemen in that long ago time when I'd searched for the missing seminarian, so I nodded.

"In Mwarai's defense, it does appear that Daniel carefully

packed the little he owned and took it away with him. There were no indications of an abduction or even any particular hurry. He said goodnight to me one evening and the next morning he was gone. But to go off like that was totally out of character for him. Out of character for anyone with his aspirations."

"His aspirations? He mentioned studying for the priesthood?"

"No," Swickard admitted. "He never did. But it wasn't all my imagination; I'm sure of that. The way he questioned me about everything, that curiosity had to have a very specific prompting. And when he assisted at Mass, the way he watched me. It reminded me of the way I'd watched the priest back when I was an altar boy, something I hadn't thought about in years."

Ruth brought in the coffee then, and Swickard brightened considerably. It was his big daily indulgence, evidently, and it was good, though very strong.

I decided that the arrival of the coffee signaled the end of dinner and the expiration of the ban on any discussion of Wauki. Even so, I approached the subject as Basil had approached the snake in the road. Circuitously.

"What was all that Wauki said about getting blood from cows? Was that just a figure of speech?"

Swickard scowled but answered me. "Not at all. Some of the herdsmen tribes have traditionally lived on cow's milk and cow's blood. They 'milk' the blood by making a small incision in the poor animal's neck."

Now that I'd spoiled his coffee, he evidently saw no point in restraining his emotions. He banged a small fist on the table and said, "Me, a tool of the government. I don't think he could have said anything that would have shocked me—hurt me—more."

I'd been thinking about the accusation myself. "Director McKenzie told me that the country's religious leaders have been asked to act as observers for the coming elections. That could look like a sellout to someone who doesn't have much faith in the process."

"It looks that way to me," Swickard said. "I think it's a case of self-delusion being inspired by self-preservation. But I don't think this Wauki was referring to any face-saving compromise worked out in Nairobi. He meant me, Philip Swickard. I've sold out.

"Twenty years of my life. . ."

I thought he was actually going to loosen up and confide in me, to tell me what hopes he'd had when he'd arrived twenty years before and what hopes he had left. He was on the verge of doing it. But he drew back.

"Having you here is making me sentimental, Owen. I would have sworn I could taste biscuits and gravy when we were talking about Midwestern food just now. And here I am about to spill my guts as though we were back at St. Aelred's and you were my spiritual advisor."

Mentioning our old seminary must have reminded the priest of Dennis Feeney. He shook his head. "Brother Dennis could not have seen this trouble coming. It isn't possible."

"It isn't logical," I said. "But then neither is Brother Dennis. As long as I'm here, I should try to find the sword."

"As long as you're here," Swickard replied, "you should make as little trouble as possible. I've some paperwork to finish up. I suggest you turn in early."

I did turn in early, but slept little, due to Ruth's strong coffee and the strange animal noises and bird calls that seemed to be coming from inside the compound walls.

My short sleep was followed by a long day. It began

with Mass, which I attended, though I ignored Swickard's side-mouthed suggestion that I assist. I sat in the back of the nearly empty church, growing as sticky over the familiar service as Swickard had gotten over biscuits and gravy the night before. I was also feeling sorry for myself. At least I was until I looked up over the altar and saw the crucified figure, whose pain seemed to contort the space around us.

After a breakfast of tea and fried dough, Swickard took me on a tour of his parish, or that tiny part of it we could visit in a day. Basil accompanied us, to keep an eye on me, it seemed. He assumed a certain proprietary air when I was approached by other children at the *shambas* where we stopped. These children always ran to Swickard first, which Basil permitted. It was a revelation to see the little priest smiling, calling out the greeting *jambo*, and patting heads.

The children's parents—most often their mothers alone were present—were more reserved around us. Around Swickard actually. I was greeted politely, as a visiting stranger, but the priest inspired a lot of downcast eyes. Clearly the word had gone out about him, though no one offered to tell us what that word had been. Without exception the farm women were working when we arrived—hoeing in garden patches, chopping wood, washing clothes or making them, even rethatching a roof—and back at it before our jeep had lurched away.

By the time we returned to the mission compound, I was as sore as if we'd made the trip on horseback. I took my leave of Swickard and Basil, thinking about a nap and a shower before the party at Chesney's. But on my way to my room I spotted Ruth in the backyard, working away like all the other women I'd seen that day. In her case the job in hand was cleaning some kind of beans. She sat on a bench with a great wooden bowl on her knees, her habitual bent posture putting her hands directly above her work.

I'd thought of Ruth more than once during our circuit of the parish. I'd had plenty of time to review my first day in Somolet, since Swickard had stuck to his practice of not speaking while he drove and Basil to his practice of not speaking much at all. One of the things I'd come back to again and again was my dinner by kerosene lamp and the look of pain that had passed over Ruth's face whenever Swickard had mentioned Daniel's name.

Her wincing had seemed natural enough at the time. The aunt was worried about the nephew. The loyal member of the mission family was troubled by the blow to Swickard's hopes for Daniel, which, for all I knew, she shared. But there had been something furtive about her reaction, too, about the way she'd done her work of clearing the table without looking at Swickard or me. It reminded me of the looks the farm women had given Swickard all day, when they'd forced themselves to look at him at all. As though they knew something he didn't and that something wasn't good.

Ruth glanced up as I approached and immediately dropped her big rheumy eyes.

"*Jambo*," I said.

She nodded.

"Need any help?"

She shook her head.

Preliminaries concluded, I dove in. "I've come to ask you something. I'd like to help my friend Father Swickard. He's worried about your nephew Daniel. I think it would help Father Philip to know why Daniel left and where he's gone. Do you know why he left?"

No check in the bean snapping.

"Do you know where Daniel's gone?"

An unsnapped bean flipped from her fingers and onto

the ground. I stooped to pick it up and stayed crouched so I could look up into her downcast eyes. She'd been crying recently. She was close to crying now.

"No one will blame you for Daniel leaving," I said. "No one will force him to come back. I'm only trying to help Father Philip."

"It will not help him," Ruth said. Her voice was slow and steady and sad. "It will hurt him."

"Hurt him how?" I restrained the impulse to start guessing, sensing that Ruth wasn't going to grant me many guesses. She was frightened, of me or of her secret. I dismissed the obvious possibilities, that Daniel had met a girl or run off to the bars and brothels of Nairobi. Neither would have provoked this reaction in his aunt. Shame, perhaps, but not fear. This had to be the product of some threat to Ruth. Or to Swickard. Wauki had been in every other thought I'd had that day, so he came to mind without effort now.

"Did Daniel run off to join Father Swickard's enemy?"

"You must promise not to tell Father Phil," Ruth said, but she was nodding almost imperceptibly as she said it.

"I promise," I said. "Now tell me. Has Daniel joined Wauki?"

"Wauki?" Ruth repeated, and I saw that I'd blundered. "Mugo," she said, her eyes filling with tears. "Daniel ran off to join Mugo."

## CHAPTER EIGHT

"It's a Sloe Gin Rickey. That's sloe gin, lime juice, fizzy water, and a slice of lime. You'll love it."

The walking bartender's guide was one of the most beautiful women I'd ever seen at close range. I'd read that the close-up was the true test of beauty, and Lorelei Praed seemed very anxious to demonstrate right off that she was up to it. The only thing that separated us was the proffered glass, and, since I was backed halfway into Chesney's aspidistra plant already, that was all there was likely to be.

She was a redhead eased toward blond by the sun, though that same sun had barely tanned the skin on her prominent cheeks. Her nose, strong as well, was slightly upturned and even more slightly freckled. Her lips were the overly full kind that actresses back in America were having injections to obtain, though Lori's—we'd already moved beyond a first-name basis to a nickname basis—had none of the shapelessness that so often resulted from human meddling.

Lori was well shaped generally, though at the range of a highball glass's diameter, I was too close to do much admiring of that. So I concentrated on her eyes, whose prominence made the rest of those prominent features work. The eyes were an ordinary brown in color, except for a distracting wedge of almost pure green radiating outward from the pupil of the right one.

"We drink a lot of gin out here, one way or another," she was saying. "It's one more cultural inheritance from the Brits. I'd say bloody Brits, but for being under dear Elizabeth's roof."

Every voice I'd heard since coming to Kenya had been exotic, Swickard's excepted. But Lori Praed's, with its very distinct Australian accent, was especially so. My Jersey accent might have seemed exotic to her, if I'd been able to say anything but "Uh huh."

I was rescued at length by Major Norris Praed, the husband. "You're melting the gentleman's ice, Lorelei," he said, putting an arm through hers and backing her up a step in the process. I took the sweating glass from her before it got away and drank gratefully.

"You'll have to forgive my wife," the major said to me. "She likes to keep in practice with the gents against the day she kicks me out. She's had your friend the padre sweating holy water any number of times."

Praed was squeezing his wife's firm arm and his tone was bantering, but his dark eyes were dead tired. The view he'd had more than his fill of might have been me or it might have been the sight of his wife flirting with any man. In either case, the solution was for me to edge away. Lori slipped off first, however, leaving me with the major.

He was taller than his tall wife and more solidly built. Also older, though he was young by my standards. Late thirties maybe. Young to be a retired soldier turned manager of a safari lodge, it seemed to me, but then I had no experience of either profession. Praed still wore his dark hair in a close-clipped military style, and his slightly receded chin was so clean-shaven that it made me self-conscious over my half day's growth. Those weary eyes of his were narrow and his lips thin, to continue the list of contrasts with Lori. Only in dress did they seem a pair, a pair of tennis pros on their day off, to be specific. Both wore shorts and matching shirts, hers a pale yellow and the major's a dustless white.

He was telling me about the Somolet Safari Lodge, which was located a little way east of the village. "On Fisher Ridge," he said. "The high ground you had to fly over to get here."

"The false escarpment?" I asked, remembering the strange term Noah had used.

"Right you are. It's called that to distinguish it from the western side of the Great Rift Valley, which is still a ways west of here. Actually, it's west and north and south, since this river valley is cut deep into the side of the true escarpment. There's wooded highland on three sides of the valley and our little ridge to the east, so the Nihuru had their peace and quiet for a long time. Their isolation didn't do them much good against the English, though, and it isn't doing them much good today."

I didn't get a chance to ask him what he meant by that. Chesney had excused her way between us.

"Sorry, Norris, but I must introduce our guest of honor to the Chief Constable. Owen, I'd like you to meet Samuel Mwarai. Samuel, this is Owen Keane, a famous detective from America."

She said it with a twinkle in her baggy eyes, which Mwarai evidently missed. "Indeed," he said with interest. "An official policeman or a private investigator?"

"Neither," said Swickard, who had broken off a conversation with the seated Rex Brocious to nose in. "Owen is a gentleman amateur. He has independent means, which allow him to investigate crimes as a hobby."

The priest hadn't taken up Chesney's joke to be entertaining. He was ribbing Mwarai, perhaps in revenge for the policeman's lack of interest in Daniel's disappearance. At the same time, he was happily putting me on the spot.

"Where's his monocle then?" Dr. Brocious demanded

from the depths of his easy chair. "If he's a gentleman sleuth, where's his monocle?"

I'd met the doctor as soon as Swickard and I had arrived. He was an overweight man in his seventies with heavy eyeglasses on a big florid face that was shiny with sweat in the relatively cool room. In addition to the glasses he wore an untucked shirt and flannel trousers, both of which may once have been white and were now unmatched grays.

Swickard had been the most formal of our party in his clerical collar, more formal even than Chesney in her floral dress, her white hair pinned up like a debutante's. But Mwarai had raised the bar slightly by showing up in uniform: khaki shorts and a sky blue shirt. The leather strap of a Sam Browne belt crossed his chest diagonally, but there was no sidearm attached to the portion of the belt that circled his very slender waist.

I'd heard him apologizing for the uniform at the door, explaining that he'd come straight from the police station. Now that we were face to face, I doubted the truth of that. His crisp shirt looked as though it'd been pressed within the hour, just after the brightwork on his shoulder boards had been polished.

Mwarai was a spare man who stood very erect, his posture emphasizing the unusual length of his neck and giving him a height advantage over everyone in the room except Praed. He also had tired-looking eyes like the major, in his case because the whites were pink. His nose was very broad and, beneath it, a shadow of moustache traced the curve of his upper lip. His chin was scarred in several places, which I decided meant that he hadn't always held his current lofty rank.

"You've solved many crimes then?" Mwarai asked me.

"I've had many investigations," I said. "A few solutions."

He nodded. "That is true the world over. Any murder

cases?"

That got everyone's attention, even the wandering Lori Praed's. She'd happened in just then to deliver another round of drinks, including Mwarai's "fizzy water," which he took straight.

"Yes," I said.

The policeman actually looked wistful. "American murder cases are so interesting. I would love to investigate one someday. Here our murders are very infrequent and very ordinary. A husband hits his wife too hard or a wife cuts her husband's throat. They don't even run and hide afterward."

"What about this banditry?" Praed asked.

Until his enthusiasm for American murders had loosened him up, Mwarai had seemed very reserved and even uncomfortable. At Praed's question, the chief constable's guard shot back up. "That is something completely different, of course. Something new."

"New to this edge of the Great Rift Valley maybe," Praed conceded.

The concession was a feint intended to cover the next jab, but the major never got to throw it. A knocking on the front door announced the arrival of the last guest, Commissioner Karari Gathitu. Chesney had described him as the local government representative, a very vague job title. He was dressed like a man of the people tonight, in a smock of a white shirt made of fabric that looked homespun, dark trousers, and sandals. Except that the shirt was collarless and its flowing sleeves cuffless, it might have been the outfit I'd left behind in Nairobi.

At odds with this simple attire was a very regal head: graying, heavy-browed, hollow-templed, and so large it made his thin frame seem boyish. This head was crowned with a plain black skullcap and adorned on the opposite end with a well-trimmed goatee, setting off a chin as square as Norris Praed's was weak. In between were sunglasses, which the commissioner didn't remove.

Gathitu's entrance subtly altered the geometry of the room. It went beyond the slight shifting toward the corners to make a space for the newcomer. Dr. Brocious went through the motions of rising. He didn't actually leave his chair, but it was more of an effort than he'd made for any of the rest of us. Mwarai virtually came to attention, and Swickard followed his example, momentarily forgetting to stoop. Lori Praed sought out her husband's arm.

Elizabeth Chesney alone seemed unaffected. She allowed Gathitu, who had been admitted by Lori, to cross the room to her. She held out her hand to him, and Gathitu took it, not bowing to kiss it but looking as though he might.

Chesney called me over then to be introduced, making no jokes this time about my reputation. Gathitu said, "A friend of Father Swickard's is always welcome." And then, to Chesney, "See? All are friends beneath your roof."

But watch out anywhere else, I decided he meant.

As soon as the introductions were out of the way, Gathitu went over to examine the spot where the Sword of Wauki had hung. The missing trophy had been the hot topic of conversation for Brocious and the Praeds when Swickard and I had entered. And I'd noticed Mwarai glancing that way before Chesney had led him over to meet me.

"Such a shame," the government man said in a very crisp but somewhat high-pitched voice. "An important historical artifact lost, perhaps forever. If only you'd turned the sword over to the government so it could have been held in trust for the people, dear Miss Chesney, as you should have done years ago. None of this would have happened. You would not now be subject to the importunities of this man who calls himself Wauki, this troublemaker."

"For all we know," Major Praed said, "the sword is in the government's hands right now. Why would anyone but the government care whether this Wauki pretender has his sword or not?"

"And why would we care?" Gathitu asked in reply.

"Because having the sword might give this Wauki bloke legitimacy. Might add to his popularity with the people."

Earlier, when she'd been full-court pressing me, the major had drawn his wife back. Now Lori returned the favor, tugging him back from his confrontation with Gathitu by saying, "What popularity, Norry? You've said yourself that Wauki is a fizzle with the common folk, that he hasn't any more followers than he can afford to keep drunk."

"Nevertheless," said Praed, who was showing some real flexibility in the matter of grievances, "we have to make sure that Elizabeth isn't victimized by this man and his threats."

"Agreed," Gathitu said. "I'm sure the chief constable will take all the necessary precautions." He addressed this to Mwarai, who nodded.

It was a chance for Swickard to reveal that Wauki's attention had shifted from Chesney to him, but the priest didn't speak. He was too stiff-necked to ask for help from Mwarai and Gathitu. I wasn't, but before I could jump in Brocious rumbled to life.

"Perhaps our new friend the amateur sleuth could shed some light on the disappearance of the sword."

All eyes turned to me, though I had to guess about Gathitu's, hidden as they were behind dark lenses.

"As a matter of fact," Chesney said, "he has an idea on the subject." She glanced around from face to face, beaming her perpetual smile. "He told me just now that the sword was taken by one of us the last time we were all together."

## CHAPTER NINE

I liked the way Chesney had distanced herself from the accusation she'd leveled against her guests, both by including
herself on the suspect list and by suggesting that the idea
had popped into my head just now, when in fact it had been
worked out with her help the day before. That little lie had
the added benefit of keeping her company from realizing
that the current get-together was a trap.

"He thinks one of us slipped in here while the rest were
in the dining room and passed the sword to a confederate
waiting outside the French doors."

Chesney didn't explain how I'd managed to discuss my
theory with her in this crowded room without anyone over-
hearing me. But no one raised that objection. They were too
busy dismissing the charge out of hand. The house was too
small for such an operation to go unnoticed. The group was
too small for someone to slip away unmissed. Reggie, in
spite of his age and infirmity, would have raised the alarm.

Eventually, though, we did get down to discussing the
business of comings and goings on the night of the original
party. Luckily the suspects decided to treat the whole thing
as a parlor game, so the atmosphere was far from strained.
The result was a lot of merry cross talk but no real prog-
ress. People had moved in and out of the trophy room all
evening, but evidently no one had been alone in there. Lori
Praed alibied Swickard and Mwarai, for instance, and they
returned the favor. Brocious and Gathitu alibied each other,

as did Major Praed and Chesney.

Dinner was eventually announced by Chesney's special-occasion cook. We gathered around an impressive table made of flame-colored wood and almost too big for the room it occupied. That room was lit by silver candelabras, which had me thinking of Christmas. I could never afterward remember much about what we ate, except that the roast was wildebeest and fussed over by everyone who tasted it. I ate little of that, haunted by the image of the upturned eye in the herd I had seen on my flight from Nairobi. Gathitu, who was seated to my right, described and recommended each dish that came, though he sampled sparingly himself and took nothing with meat in it. Wauki was still the main subject of conversation, but there were playful asides on the social evils of amateur detecting tossed back and forth by Brocious and Swickard.

After one of these volleys, Gathitu said to me, "If you'd met our so-called Wauki, you would not be looking for a sword thief among this good company. You would know where the guilt lies."

"I have met him," I said, which got me center stage again. "He came to the mission yesterday afternoon to threaten Father Swickard."

Expressions of concern followed from everyone. Directed to Swickard, of course, who was too busy glowering at me to acknowledge them.

"Threatened him how?" Gathitu inquired. It was a question Mwarai might have asked, but the policeman was deferring to the government man completely.

"He believes Father Swickard has the sword. He threatened to search the mission if the sword isn't turned over to him."

"The high-handedness we've come to expect from that impostor," the commissioner said. "Anything else?"

There was the charge of duplicity Wauki had made against

Swickard, but if I mentioned that I'd be looking for a place to sleep. "He said something about the lords in Nairobi trying to steal the land of the people."

I said that as innocently as Chesney had earlier introduced my theory about the stolen sword, and with the same secret expectation of a brouhaha. I almost got one.

Major Praed cooperated: "Just shows that Wauki isn't all hot air. The land grabbing's old news up north in the big valley. Now it's our turn down here."

But Gathitu spotted the trap this time. He ignored the Australian and concentrated on me. "You're surely not pretending, Mr. Keane, that Father Swickard hasn't told you all about our land problems. It's his favorite sermon topic, from what I'm told."

"He mentioned that someone was encouraging friction between the tribes as a way of acquiring land."

"You were very politic for once in your choice of words, Father, if in fact those were your words."

"They weren't," Swickard said.

"Did you also give your friend the government's position in this unfortunate situation, in the interest of fairness?"

"I did not."

"I'd like to hear it," I said.

"Very well," Gathitu said. "As you may know, Kenya is a land of many ethnic groups, which some of my less progressive compatriots insist on calling tribes. The English took land from all of them, indiscriminately, judging only the suitability of the land itself and disregarding any group's ancient rights to it. When independence came, a great deal of land was returned to the people. Unfortunately, insufficient care was taken to see that it was returned to the correct people, by which I mean to the correct ethnic group. In many cases, the land went to the native Kenyans who had been working it for the English, but these were not always members of the local indigenous population. They were often individuals brought in from another part of the country because of a certain skill, tending cattle say, or because they were more tractable or westernized than the local people.

"The situation we are experiencing now, which Father Swickard and others see as the result of secret government machinations, is merely the redistribution of the land to reflect the original ownership. If violence is occurring or if some unscrupulous individuals are taking advantage of the situation to acquire land for themselves, well, those are just unhappy byproducts of the process."

"It's no secret," Swickard said in rebuttal, "that the current government encourages tribalism as a way of keeping the people divided into controllable factions. If instead an effort were made to persuade every Kenyan to think of himself as a Kenyan first and a member of an ethnic group second, there'd be no excuse for this violence. Of course, then we might see new faces in the government come election day."

No one said anything to that. I looked to Chesney to step in and found that she was looking back at me with an expression that said, "It's your party."

I started with Praed. "Didn't you tell me, Major, that the Nihuru are fairly isolated here?"

"That's right, they are."

"Did the British settlers bring many members of other tribes—I mean, ethnic groups—into this valley?"

"No," Chesney said. "The Nihuru were skilled herdsmen, and they became splendid farmers. They're successful at anything they turn their hands to."

Gathitu accepted the compliment with a nod.

"Then where," I asked, "does the threat of friction come from?"

"Where indeed," Gathitu said.

"There are isolated farms owned by non-Nihuru," Swickard said.

"And there's this banditry," the major cut in. "Mr. Gathitu didn't mention that." I could feel his wife, seated to my left, kicking at him beneath the table. He didn't miss a beat. "Armed gangs in the employ of God knows who are scaring the farmers off their land. They've been moving this way for months."

"Rumors only," Gathitu said. "Rumors fueled by the random acts of poachers. Have you heard anything of this, Chief Constable?"

Mwarai started. "We have no poachers in the valley," he said.

"We were speaking of bandits," Gathitu said sharply.

"I have seen none," Mwarai said, confirming his reputation as a careful man.

Chesney finally decided that we'd had enough playtime. "So interesting that you had a chance to meet Wauki," she said to me. "Did he tell you anything about himself? Where he came from perhaps?"

"No. He told me how the original Wauki died. It was the basic situation you'd described. But he came off better in his version."

"He would," said Brocious, who'd been drinking himself scarlet on Chesney's wine.

"And he closed with something interesting. Something I didn't follow. He said he'd returned before."

"Yes," Chesney said thoughtfully. "I seem to remember something about that in connection with one of the Mau Mau leaders. You've heard of the Mau Mau, Owen?"

"The terrorist group?" I asked. Lori kicked *me* this time, though it was really more of a healthy poke.

"The group that led the struggle for Kenyan independence," Chesney amended, which won her another nod from Gathitu. "The history of the Mau Mau is one of your areas of interest, is it not, Doctor?" she said to Brocious.

"Every part of Kenya's history is of interest to me," he said, rousing himself.

"Do you remember anything about Wauki's previous reincarnation?"

"Of course. It was a claim made by — or more likely made on behalf of — one of the Mau Mau leaders. A man named Bonosoi. He was executed by the British, as some say Wauki was. As to Bonosoi actually being Wauki, I don't think anyone took that too seriously. For one thing, he wasn't a Nihuru. He was a Kikuyu, as were most of the Mau Mau. They're close cousins to the Nihuru, but still. No, Bonosoi's Wauki linkage was something on the order of the Tudors' claim to be descendants of King Arthur or an American president's boast that he was born in a log cabin. Something only the simplest follower would believe."

It was the longest speech I'd heard from the doctor and the first serious one. It was delivered clearly, wine and gin notwithstanding, and without a break beyond the second it took him to push his glasses back up his sweating nose.

Brocious seemed even soberer later as he and I sat on the back verandah overlooking the moonlit garden, though by then he was drinking brandy. Gathitu and Mwarai had gone, as had the Praeds. Swickard and Chesney still sat with their heads together at the beautiful dining room table. Our third on the verandah was Reggie, released from his captivity and sprawled on the cool stone between us. The doctor had told me of his birthplace, an English village called Stow-on-the-Wold, and was now summing up a lecture on the beauties of his adopted country.

"I love this place. Everyone you met tonight does, in his own way. Her own way. Even the Praeds, though they've been here less than a year, which you wouldn't guess from that puppy major's tendency to talk like an old hand. I knew plenty like him during the war, officers no older than I was but full of the wisdom of ages. Dangerous men."

A distant animal call came to us. It sounded like someone gargling through a tuba.

Reggie sat up at the sound, and Brocious put a meaty hand on his collar. "Steady, old boy. Hear that, Owen? That's a lion poking about. Don't often hear one this close to the village. You may be the first one of your line to hear a lion in the wild for a hundred generations. A thousand perhaps."

"I may be the first period," I said. "I'm Irish."

"Actually, you're most likely a Kenyan, Owen. That's what the archeologist chaps tell us. Mankind got its start right here in Kenya, or just south of us in Tanzania. 'And the Lord God planted a garden eastward in Eden,' as my old mum's bible put it. This could be that very garden.

"Of course, it isn't paradise any longer. We're here. Modern Man is here, with all our vast capacity for mischief. You don't suppose God actually cast us out of the Garden, do you? That was just literary license on the part of some Old Testament scribbler. What He did was cast the Garden out of us. Or—if you believe in free will—we cast it out of ourselves. We plucked the pure simple goodness out of ourselves. And we've had to live with what was left. We've built our poor world with what was left inside us.

"Still, you occasionally come upon pockets of that old primeval goodness. They're like the patches of the old tropical forest you find here and there on the savanna. I've found more than my share of those pure hearts here in Kenya.

"How about you, old chap? Have you ever met a person

like that? A throwback to the old pure goodness?"

"One," I said. "She was killed by a drunk driver."

"Well naturally," Brocious said.

## CHAPTER TEN

The next day started as a duplicate of the one before, except that the jeep tour was shorter and skirted an area of tea plantations whose hillside fields were the greenest things I'd seen in Kenya. We were back in time for a lunch of *githeri*, which was mostly corn and beans. Swickard tucked away dangerous quantities.

After lunch I sat on the front porch with my trusty guide-book, reading the section on the Mau Mau uprising and fighting sleep. It was very still. The clothesline load, which now included some things of mine, was perfectly motionless. I'd nearly dropped off when Swickard came out wearing his patched straw hat. He announced that he was visiting a sick parishioner and I wasn't, since he didn't want me catching something that might lay me up in Somolet for weeks. I thought he might actually just be tired of baby-sitting tourists, but I didn't argue. Our relationship had been less enjoyable than ever since the party. The priest told me to stay put, said he meant it this time, and roared off in the jeep.

I looked around for Ruth. I wanted to tackle her again on the subject of Mugo, but she was off to market. I learned this from Basil, who was keeping my shadow company as usual.

He offered to take me to Somolet proper, the site of the market, and I accepted the offer, thinking that a friendly call on Chief Constable Mwarai might be in order. Away from Major Praed's aggressiveness and Commissioner Gathitu's supervision, the careful policeman might actually consent to a conversation.

We took the unpaved road that led to Chesney's. The village was a little way beyond her turnoff, a collection of mud-colored buildings of which Mwarai's police station was the largest. The inside of the station was brightly lit and as clean as Swickard's very clean house. We were informed by a constable who might have been a smallpox survivor that his boss was out on patrol and not expected back soon.

Nor was Ruth anywhere in the vicinity of the little market. The market had a faded Coca-Cola sign, but none of the actual product. I bought Basil and me a round of ginger beers, and we sat on a bench under an umbrella tree until some old men claimed squatters' rights. Then we headed back.

Not far from the village we came upon a man standing in the center of the road. He was almost as old as the ones who had chased us off Somolet's only park bench. He was gray-bearded and wore a shapeless red hat, a remarkably red hat, given that the rest of him was as dusty as Basil and I had gotten on our walk.

As we approached him he began to talk very rapidly. I'd left my guidebook and its Swahili/English dictionary back at the mission, not that I was even sure the man was speaking Swahili. Luckily, Basil was on the job.

"He says his name is Tot," Basil told me in the voice I'd grown to like so well, the voice that was half little boy's, half tenured professor's. "He says he's been to the mission to find the priest but the priest wasn't there."

"*Jambo*," I said. I was going to add that Swickard would be back around five, but the old man began speaking again, so tonelessly that I wondered if he might be partially deaf.

"He says he knows where the sword is," Basil translated. "The Sword of Wauki. He says he's seen it."

Tot spoke again.

"He knows the mission is in danger because of the sword. He wants to help the little man. He means Father Philip."

"Ask him to describe the sword."

Tot stooped and drew a line in the dust of the road. It was about the right length, the length of the discolored space on Chesney's wall. Even better, the line was distinctly curved, which is how Chesney had described the cutlass's blade.

"Ask him to tell us where the sword is."

That was a mistake. Tot's reply was to start down the road toward the village, talking as he went.

"He says he'll take us there for a shilling. It's at a farm a little way from here."

I liked the shilling part. It was a more tangible motive than Tot's stated concern for the mission. But I wasn't as warm to the idea of just walking in on whoever had taken the sword. Not with Basil along. I asked for more information on that point.

"Nice people. Good people," was how Basil translated the answer. There was no question how he voted. He was following Tot, hitching up his tattered shorts. "Give me the shilling," he said. "I will bring back the sword."

I looked toward the mission and then toward Chesney's, which was much closer. Tot, a hundred yards away now, was leaving the road for a side path that ran in the opposite direction from Chesney's lane.

"Damn," I said and ran to catch up.

We descended a gentle slope that was clear enough of trees to give us a view that stretched for miles. The path was narrow but free of grass, suggesting that it was a minor Somolet thoroughfare. Still, we never saw another soul. We saw no animals either but found many of their tracks and droppings. Basil identified each pile of the latter in an offhand, old scout way.

The dangerous sun was finally getting well down in the sky, which at that stage of the expedition I took to be a good thing, since it meant cooler walking. We came to a branching of the path, Tot striking off to his left at a vigorous pace, me lagging behind to memorize the turning. There was nothing much to memorize. I asked Basil if he was sure he could find his way back, which strained our friendship.

"Of course," he said, tapping his narrow chest with a tiny fist.

I asked him again when the path met a narrow road and again when we traded that road for another. By then he was only waving a hand in reply. He was still dutifully translating the questions I directed to Tot. Actually one question, repeated at half hour intervals: "How much farther?" The relayed answer was always, "Not far."

We passed a succession of little farms, sometimes attracting the attention of children and dogs, sometimes raising the head of a cow or two. None was the farm we were after. Although it was no time for it, I began slipping into my state of mental detachment again. It was a defense mechanism, after all, so it was natural that I'd fall back on it now as a refuge from my nerves. My walking doze was aided by what was now the light of early evening. It had a golden quality I'd always associated with autumn afternoons. Our road was following some tributary of the Nihuru through a glade of trees whose fern-like leaves cast a tracery of shadows as delicate as lace at our feet. I studied the shifting patterns, forgetting to ask for updates, forgetting to mark our way.

When Tot finally called a halt and began to speak, I was almost irritated at the interruption. Basil said, "He wants his shilling. There is the house. The sword is inside."

I shook my head, both to clear it and as a visual aid. "First the sword, then the shilling."

The house was a sturdy looking ranch with the steel roof upgrade. Smoke curled above the roof, not from a chimney but from a fire behind the house. The small yard was surrounded by a field of stunted corn. When we drew closer, I saw that the yard was further set off by a rough fence of thorny branches woven between upright stakes. I stopped us when we reached an open gate in this perimeter.

"How many inside?" I asked.

"Two," Tot said through Basil. "Nice people."

"Call them."

That never happened. Our haggling at the gate had already attracted the residents, a man and a woman, neither young.

Tot greeted them and then addressed me. Basil said, "They speak English."

"Good evening," I said. "We've come about the sword."

Immediately the couple's expressions changed from mild apprehension to extreme pleasure. "Of course," the man called and waved us up.

Tot demanded his shilling again. I passed it to Basil, who slapped it into the old man's palm.

We scattered chickens on our way across the yard, bypassing a goat who indicated with a slightly lowered head that he had no intention of scattering.

An exchange of names took place on the rickety front stoop. Its owners were the Ngatinis, George and Mai. George was the shorter and wider of the two, and the cut of his untucked shirt suggested bowling to my New Jersey eye. Mai wore a dress and kerchief made from the same rose colored print.

Coming out of his third or fourth bow, George asked me, "How did you hear about the sword?"

I turned to look for Tot and saw his red hat bobbing above the field of maize as he hurried off the way we'd come. By then the Ngatinis were ushering us inside, George actually leading me by the hand to the sword itself.

It hung above a heavy wooden shelf that looked like a hunting lodge mantel but lacked a fireplace underneath. The sword—less than three feet in length and slightly curved—wore a brightly polished metal scabbard that was wound around in several places with cords of red and yellow silk. Rising from the scabbard was a flat handle of carved wood topped by what looked like a golden sea urchin.

It was a Japanese samurai sword, a beautiful thing, but as unlike a British naval cutlass as it could possibly be.

George, oblivious to my disappointment, was giving me its history. "My father, Benjamin Ngatini"—he indicated a black and white photo on the mantel shelf—"served with the British army in the Second World War, here in Africa and later in Burma. Do you know Burma?"

"I know of it."

"Very bad jungle, the worst my father had ever seen. Tigers and many Japanese. My father took the sword in battle. Killed the Japanese officer who carried it, though he was wounded himself. The British gave him a medal."

He took a box from the shelf and showed me the decoration, a white enameled cross with a golden crown at its center on a ribbon of red and blue. "And they sent him back here. His officer, Colonel Chesney, kept the sword because he knew that my father, a simple man, would have given it to the first stranger who asked him for it. After the war, Colonel Chesney brought the sword to my father himself and saluted him. He was a fine gentleman, the colonel."

"I've met his daughter," I said.

"Yes, yes. Miss Elizabeth. She was my first teacher."

That gave me an opening to verify that Tot had in fact wasted my time. "Miss Chesney lost a sword recently." George had already heard that news. "You haven't by any chance seen it, have you?"

"Sadly no. It would be a great honor to return it to her. To repay her for the service her father did for my father."

Mai was bustling about us with glasses and a bottle, working with her left hand only and supporting the right one in the binding of her apron. George explained that she'd only recently had her wrist removed from a cast following an altercation with the goat, which confirmed my first impression of that animal.

"Will you drink a toast to my father?" George asked me.

"I'd be honored," I said, speaking in the singular on the assumption that Basil would be exempted. But he got his glass along with the rest of us. A pause followed. Then I noticed Basil nodding at me and realized that I was toastmaster.

"To the memory of a brave soldier," I said. "Benjamin Ngatini."

The colorless liquid was like vodka without the playfulness.

"*Changa'a*," George said. "Mai makes the best you'll find."

Basil evidently thought so. He was smacking his lips in appreciation. Next George invited us to share their dinner.

"We've a long walk back," I began and again noticed Basil's head moving, this time from side to side.

"A long walk," he said, "which will be shorter after a good meal."

I thought the boy might just be hungry or hoping for another shot of moonshine. He cleared things up for me as George and Mai prepared our places. "Bad manners to go without eating."

Dinner turned out to be my second helping of *githeri* that day. The Ngatinis served it with flat bread that they broke into pieces and used as a spoon. I had to admit, it did taste better that way. We sat behind the little house on a massive stone slab, enjoying the last of a blood red sunset.

At one point in the meal, George said, "If we'd known you would be here, Owen, we would have killed the goat."

I took this as a polite exaggeration, since sacrificing even a chicken would have been a considerable extravagance. The goat in question, standing nearby, took it as a genuine threat and stared holes in me.

It was fully dark by the time we'd finished eating. George asked if we wanted to stay the night. I checked my Kenyan Emily Post, by which I mean I consulted Basil. "*Asante*," he said, "but we have a moon."

That George didn't try to talk us out of the walk back reassured me, as did Basil's complete insouciance. And he was right about the moon, which was nearly full. It was low in the sky and huge as we started our walk. It rose quickly, losing size but gaining candlepower until we were casting shadows by it, Basil's as straight-backed as Colonel Chesney in his portrait.

The insect noises were as amazing as the moon, louder by far than anything I'd heard in New Jersey, louder even than the buzzing fields I'd encountered in the Midwest. I wondered if Swickard grew nostalgic listening to the sound, but I didn't dwell on it. I found any thought of the priest unpleasant, knowing as I did that I was in for a verbal beating when we finally got back to the mission. If we'd come back with the sword, I could have dodged that. Now I'd just have to stand up under it.

Basil might have been thinking the same thing. Except for the occasional burp, he was his usual quiet self. I didn't prod him to talk. I was aware that he was listening intently to the night sounds and I didn't want to jam the frequency. He paused only once, at a distant yelping that sounded like one scalded dog arguing with another. When the sounds faded, we resumed our tramp.

Basil definitely heard the truck before I did. We'd walked almost an hour at that point, and I'd begun to worry about finding the path that led up to the mission road. Basil stopped and turned and then I heard it, too, the sound of a motor in low gear. While we stood waiting I had time to ask myself why the sound of a vehicle approaching at night on a dark road was more frightening than any of the animal noises I'd heard.

Before I'd come up with an answer, the truck rounded a bend and its headlights caught us squarely. I didn't bother waving it down. I never even considered the possibility that it would pass us by.

The vehicle — a Land Rover — stopped right beside us with an angry squeal of brakes. Major Praed leaned out its open side. "Owen! By God, I thought you had more sense than this. Get in double-quick. All hell's broken loose. Wauki's been hacked to death, and that's not the worst of it. They've arrested your mate, the padre, for the murder."

# CHAPTER ELEVEN

Praed the military man must have had some training in giving cogent reports. He gave me one as soon as we were rolling.

"Philip rang the lodge about six looking for you. Guess he was calling everyone he could think of trying to find you. Ten minutes later he called back to see if I'd go out to search for you. He was going himself, and he'd dragooned old Doc Brocious, too. He gave me a patch to cover and told me to report to the mission at eight win or lose and we'd go from there.

"It was quarter past eight when I actually got to the mission. Mwarai and a squad of his men were there. The padre had called them after finding the body. Wauki — I guess we're stuck calling him that now — was sprawled on the mission's front steps, hacked about the head and neck, blood everywhere. I've seen cleaner work from a machete.

"Mwarai was putting the arm on the padre as I walked up. I couldn't talk him out of it, and I got pretty warm trying. Lucky thing Doc Brocious arrived then and broke up the argument, or I might have landed in the nick myself. I slipped away to have another go at finding you."

"Why would Mwarai arrest Father Philip?"

"He called it protective custody, but I don't believe him. I kicked it around just now after I'd calmed a little and came up with two possibilities. One is that Mwarai doesn't really think the padre's guilty but sees this as a chance to put a know-it-all foreigner on ice while the election plays out.

Mwarai isn't political, but he knows who signs his paychecks."

"Could he be following Gathitu's orders?"

"I don't think so. His nibs flew to Nairobi this morning. Mwarai can't have had time to put a call through yet."

"What's the second possibility?"

"Mwarai really believes that Philip did it. God help us then."

Without my noticing how, the major had gotten us onto the upper road. The mission compound was right ahead, its front lit by the headlights of more jeeps and trucks than I would have guessed Somolet possessed. The major drove through the open car gate and parked next to the other vehicles in the front yard.

Mwarai was still in personal command, which he demonstrated as soon as we pulled up. He barked an order to a uniformed man, who trotted to Praed's Land Rover and extracted Basil.

"Doesn't want the little chap to see the gore," Praed whispered to me. But as Basil was led off to the dormitory, the boy never even glanced toward the crime scene. He was too busy staring back at me like he'd never see me again.

Dr. Brocious stood beside Mwarai, smoking a cigarette, his soiled Panama hat well back on his head. The man I was poised to defend, Philip Swickard, was nowhere to be seen.

Wauki, on the other hand, was still very much a presence. I'd hoped he'd have been taken away, in the discreet way bodies exited on television shows, under a blanket or a sheet or in a bag. Instead, he lay sprawled facedown on the front steps—the steps he'd once used as a stage—his arms stretched wide on either side. His gaping wounds, only slightly darkened by the warm night air, were attracting the eager attention of night-shift flies. A constable, whose uniform was similar to Mwarai's but topped with a beret, had been detailed to fend them off with a bamboo whisk. He looked as sick as I felt.

My nausea came in part from imagining my own body sprawled there on the steps. This should have been you, I told myself. This is what you came to Somolet to find.

"Ahem," Mwarai said to call the meeting to order. "And where have you been, Mr. Keane?"

"Having dinner at the *shamba* of George and Mai Ngatini," I said readily, having practiced the answer on Praed. For no reason other than nerves, I added, "They're friends of Miss Chesney's."

I was surprised to see that that dubious claim impressed the policeman. His expression softened markedly, and his stiff neck seemed to retract an inch or two. I'd never get a better moment to speak up for Swickard.

"Chief Constable, what's become of Father Philip?"

"I've had him sent to Somolet in protective custody. As I tried to explain to Major Praed, the priest would not be safe here once word of this gets out."

"But you can't believe he's involved in any way."

"I've only just begun my investigation. Dr. Brocious was giving me his report. Doctor."

Brocious took the cigarette from his drooping lips, flicked the ash away, and placed it back. "My preliminary report," he corrected. "Though I doubt I'll find anything important when I get a chance to examine him thoroughly. You have the murder weapon, of course.

"The missing cutlass," Brocious added for my benefit. "The victim was attacked from behind and struck, I would say, twelve times. The first blow killed him. The remainder were done out of pure hatred."

"How do you know the first blow killed him?" Mwarai asked.

Brocious looked to me. I said, "From the position of the

91

body. Wauki made no attempt to block his fall or to fight off the subsequent blows."

"Very good," the doctor said. "Your men will bring me the corpse fairly soon, Chief Constable? Before it comes to life again, this time with maggots?"

"Directly," Mwarai said. "Perhaps, Mr. Keane, you would like to examine the scene before it is disturbed. There is much blood splatter evidence. You will find that of interest, I am sure."

"I am not," I muttered.

I would have said no in much plainer language than that, but Praed put his hand on my shoulder. "For the padre's sake, Owen."

"Mind the blood, splattered and otherwise," Brocious said. "I needn't remind you of AIDS, I'm sure."

I walked over to the steps. It wasn't much of a trip, but during the course of it I moved backward in time two years, my head filling up with images of a posh hotel room in Boston where a single shot had blown much of a young woman's head away. They were memories I'd suppressed with great success, at least during my waking hours. I fought them back now, afraid I'd break down in front of Mwarai and the others as I had that night.

Brocious, at my elbow, had spotted my struggle. "Cigarette, old chap?" he asked. "They help a little. With the smell, I mean. I've never gotten used to the smell of violent death. The smells, I should say. That's the thing the cinema never gets right. They ladle on the blood these days, I'm told, but without the smell of it, and of feces and urine, movie death is still too idealized, too glamorized."

By then he'd gotten the cigarette in my hand and lit. My first for years and years.

Major Praed was covering for me, too, by confronting

Mwarai in his usual agreeable way. "You can't leave this body here much longer, Chief Constable. Or the blood. You'll have half the lions in the district nosing about. The old women and the children won't be safe."

"The women and children will not be here for long either," Mwarai replied. "I intend to take them away when we leave. The brother of the cook will provide for them if I ask him."

"They'll need to be guarded," Praed said. "From Wauki's men."

"From the murderer," I murmured.

"I will detail a guard," Mwarai said, "but the children saw and heard nothing. They were at their dinner in their building behind the main house, the old cook and the housekeeper with them. After dark, that is. While it was light, the little ones were playing in the yard. So the murder must have occurred just after dark."

He looked to Brocious, who said, "Sounds reasonable. And the fact that the children heard nothing supports our theory that the first blow killed him, Owen." He drew me as close to the body as I intended to get. "I think it was this one, the one that nearly severed his head."

I remembered again the plan that had brought me to Kenya. The plan to stretch my neck so far someone would be tempted to sever it. A metaphorical plan, but here it was in sliced flesh and hacked bone.

Brocious was rumbling on. "You can see that the other wounds are completely different in shape. They were struck with downward blows, like you'd use if you were hacking at an old stump. The body had fallen by then. But this first blow was struck with an upward motion."

"The blow of a short man reaching upward," Mwarai said. "Like the little priest."

"I suppose," the doctor conceded.

The famous cutlass lay nearby, and I moved to it gratefully, though it was a grisly object itself, blood drying everywhere on its heavy blade and on the dull brass of the guard. "The murderer must have been covered with blood," I said.

Brocious got academic on me, which wasn't helpful. "Less blood than you'd suppose. The first blow killed, remember. After that the blood had no motive force of its own. The violence of the subsequent blows dispersed a certain quantity, but most of what you see around you simply seeped out."

Mwarai was as confused as I was. "But the assailant would have been struck by some of the blood."

"Oh certainly."

"Was there any blood on Father Swickard?" I asked.

The chief constable said, "He had an hour from sunset until the time he reported the body to clean himself."

"He would have left traces of that in the mission."

"Not necessarily, Mr. Keane. The Nihuru River is only a short walk from here. The killer could have gone there to remove the blood."

"If he wasn't afraid of crocodiles," Brocious said in a loud aside.

"He couldn't have cleaned bloodstains from his clothes in that brown muck," Praed challenged.

"Then we'll find bloodstained clothing," Mwarai answered with determination. "I've sent a man to walk the path to the river."

I'd stooped to examine the sword more closely. The blade was wider and heavier than I'd been picturing it. Praed had compared the cutlass to a machete, but to me it more resembled a cleaver, not in the shape of the blade but in the mass of metal backing up the cutting edge. At its tip, the cutlass's blade was miraculously free of blood. I borrowed a match from the doctor and examined the weapon's edge at that point. It glinted like it had just come from the forge.

"This has been sharpened since it was stolen," I said.

"Very like," Praed said. "But what of it? This is farming country, Owen. The humblest *shamba* has a stone for sharpening tools."

The mission didn't, not that I'd seen, but I didn't raise the point. I could guess Mwarai's answer. The sword had been missing for weeks, time enough for Swickard to have sharpened it with whatever tools were on hand or to have had it done by some loyal parishioner at some remote farm.

We were interrupted at that point by the return of Mwarai's scout. On the end of a long knife he carried a pair of cotton work gloves, stiff with blood. The essence of the constable's report was passed to me by his boss.

"Found between here and the river, as one would expect. It's too dark to conduct a proper search, even with the moon. We'll resume at first light.

"Doctor, you may supervise the removal of the body if you wish. Sergeant, inform the women that the children must be ready to leave at once."

I was last on the orders list. "Mr. Keane, I'm afraid you must relocate as well. I could put you up at the station."

He made the offer in a friendly way, but I could almost hear again the hollow clang of the Nairobi police van's door. Praed stepped in.

"He's welcome to stay with us at the lodge. We've a empty cottage." Under his breath, he added, "That's all we'll have this time tomorrow."

"Very well," Mwarai said. "Should I require any further information from you gentlemen, I will call upon you there."

## CHAPTER TWELVE

The next morning a vision brought me orange juice. She wore a yellow bikini, the lower half of which peeked out through a slit in her wet-towel skirt. The orange juice wore a very plain glass supported by a silver tray a little bigger than a coaster.

"Morning, Okie," Lorelei Praed called while she was still some way off. "Did you sleep at all?"

During our discussion of nicknames at Chesney's dinner party, I'd impulsively mentioned "Okie," the name Brother Dennis had invented for me back in the seminary and still used. That echo of the monk should have been a call to arms, a reminder that the man he'd sent me to Africa to help was in jail, but the bugle call had to compete for my attention with the shimmer of morning sunlight on wet red hair.

I was seated in a canvas chair overlooking a little pond that itself overlooked the Nihuru Valley. Behind me was my "cottage," a circular pseudo hut with a conical thatched roof. I'd had a chance to study the roof at some length, since it was also the ceiling above the hut's single bed. That ceiling was supported by a series of cedar beams, between which ran concentric rings of tightly woven mats, each mat, I estimated, two feet in width. What sort of reeds or stalks or leaves the mats were woven from, hours of sleepless observation hadn't divulged.

"I slept a little," I said.

"A very little, I bet." She walked with the easy grace I'd

noticed in Kenyan women on the streets of Nairobi, and I wondered if she'd picked it up from them or brought it with her from Sydney. "Sleeping next to Norry was like sharing a bed with a stack of teacups. The least little move out of me and crash."

It was a totally innocent remark, meant only to convey Praed's nervous tension, but the primary result was to start me picturing Lori in bed. Worse distractions followed.

"Did you bring a bathing suit? 'Cause I wanted to warn you not to swim in the pond. Don't swim in any still water hereabouts; you can catch snail fever. Our pool's okay, of course. Did you see it when Norry slipped you in last night?"

"I didn't bring a suit."

"You can borrow one of Norry's. Or you could swim without one. We had some Germans here last month who insisted on doing that. Don't know whether it was their natural practice or they thought it was the African thing to do. I joined in, but I never really felt comfortable. You have to change your tanning regimen for something like that."

Or start one, I thought. She was close enough by then—seated opposite me on the canvas footstool that went with my chair—for me to see that no part of her was particularly tanned. When I caught myself beginning my second inspection pass, I dove into the orange juice. It was very cold. The little metal saucer Lori had carried it out on had come straight from a freezer powered by the lodge's very own electric generator.

I'd noticed many little five-star touches like that at the Somolet Safari Lodge, in part because Major Praed had called my attention to them the night before. He'd brought me a bottle of very nice scotch, mumbled something about its being a better nightcap than "goddamn chocolates on your goddamn pillow," and stomped off. I'd been left with the impression that he was somehow embarrassed by the place.

"Have you been happy here?" I asked his wife.

"Middling happy," she said. "One day was pretty like another until these bloody elections were called."

Even when she discussed a serious subject she was sexy. Now, for example, as she gave my question more thought, she ran a thumb inside one strap of her bathing suit top, absentmindedly easing its not inconsiderable load.

"Overall," she said, "I think it's better than I expected it to be. I didn't know what to expect really. But I love the lodge and I've gotten to love Somolet, bump in the outback that it is.

"Norry though. I think he was disappointed, at least at first. Kept calling himself a bloody innkeeper. I think he was hoping for something rougher. Someplace where he could go around decorated with rifle cartridges, with a big knife in his belt, playing the great white hunter. Something like the army. Something dangerous and exciting."

She sighed. "But then the election bother started and Norry brightened up overnight. He loves the idea of the good guys and the bad guys squaring off and everyone with a secret agenda."

"What did he think of Wauki?"

"Oh, Wauki was the biggest plum in his pudding at first. Norry was sure there'd be trouble over him and his fairy story. But no real trouble came. Until last night, I mean. Wauki never got on that well with the Nihuru.

"I'm sorry he's dead," she added. "He was always nice to me, though his eyes had a tendency to roam when he spoke to me."

My own eyes happened to be fixed on hers at that moment. In an effort to keep them there, I narrowed my focus even further, concentrating on the rogue wedge of green in her right eye.

"And I'm truly sorry Father Phil is in trouble over it," she continued. "I sure can't picture him hacking anyone to death."

"Who can you picture doing it?"

She said, "No one," but returned at once to the subject of her warrior husband. "Okie, promise me you'll keep Norry from doing anything wild. I'm half afraid he'll try to break Father Phil out of jail. I know Philip wouldn't want that. You're older than Norry. You can steady him. You and Elizabeth."

I was simultaneously irritated at being lumped into the same generation as the white-haired Chesney and amused by the idea that I could advise the tough-guy major. Lori ran her thumb along her bikini's strap a second time, tilting the decision in her favor.

"I'll be happy to help you steady him," I said.

She sighed again. "I won't be around to help. Norry's decided we should pack our current guests—some French engineers—off early. You see, this place is one of a string of lodges owned by the same big outfit. Our guests make the grand tour of Kenya by moving from one lodge to the next. This lot was due to transfer to a place on the Maasai Mara later in the week. Norry's decided that they're to go today and me with them. He doesn't want me around should real trouble break."

When she stood up, her wet towel stayed on the canvas stool. She retrieved it and slung it over one lightly freckled shoulder.

I said, "What will Chief Constable Mwarai say to your leaving?"

She laughed. "You mean when he loses one of his prime suspects? A tennis racket's more my weapon. Samuel Mwarai won't mind. I'm more worried about Commissioner Gathitu. I'm never quite sure about him. I can't see his eyes through those sunglasses he always wears. I go a lot by a person's eyes."

She took a moment to consider mine, but didn't announce her findings. "I've a good alibi for yesterday evening," she said. "It was my job to baby-sit the Frenchies while Norry was out hunting for you. We sat up till all hours playing cards. Poker, which they're no good at. They wanted to make it strip poker, but I had no desire to see the lot of them naked. But I couldn't get them to stop playing either. That's why I wasn't able to welcome you properly last night.

"I'll make up for it with breakfast this morning."

She cut herself off and adjusted the same bathing suit strap with the same thumb for the third time. By then I'd decided that the strap business was what gamblers call a "tell," a bit of body language or a nervous habit that reveals something about the doer's mental state. In Lori's case, the tell was a tip-off that a thoughtful remark was coming.

"Don't misjudge Kenya by this fracas, Okie. It's not Rwanda by a long chalk, with one tribe murdering off another. Father Phil and Norry are afraid it could come to that, if the big men in Nairobi overplay their divide and conquer game. But I don't think it will. There's too much good in the Kenyan heart."

"Dr. Brocious said almost the same thing."

"Did he? Well, good on him. The old sot's got a soft center, that's for certain. He still makes house calls, do you believe it? And him seventy-five if he's a day. Guess you have to get about when your patients are scattered like the lost tribes. He's seen a lot, our doctor. And stayed around for more.

"Now, what about those eggs?"

"I'm not sure I can eat much this morning," I said.

"You'd better try. Once I'm gone, the mad major may have you on hard tack and field rations."

## CHAPTER THIRTEEN

After breakfast, I used the lodge's very reliable satellite phone to place a call to Director McKenzie in Nairobi. He might have already heard the bad news, since he wasn't available to take my call. His efficient secretary took a message, but this time she didn't bother to read it back. I hung up wondering whether she'd even written it down.

Later I helped Major Praed load his wife's things and the baggage of the French engineers into the larger of the lodge's two Land Rovers. He did the last bit of loading himself, slipping a rifle in beside the driver's seat. I'd noted the prior evening that he'd traded in his tennis pro's whites for a soldier's olive drab. He carried a second rifle slung over his shoulder, where it looked quite natural. He gave Lori a very chaste kiss and then looked on darkly while she kissed me, even more chastely, on the cheek. Then the major and I set off for Somolet.

We got in to see Swickard without any difficulty, though we actually had to go in, the constable on duty being unwilling to bring the priest out. We joined him in his cell, where he was finishing his breakfast, a bowl of some kind of meal. I felt guilty all over again about the second helpings I'd enjoyed at the lodge. Swickard had other offenses of mine to discuss.

"Owen," he started in as soon as the guard had locked up Praed and me and left, "my own personal Judas. The man who's delivered me to my enemies. I called you congenitally immature before and felt bad about it. Now I know I was letting you off too easily. You're not just backward; you're malevolent. You enjoy making trouble, especially where the priesthood is concerned."

"Easy, Padre," Praed interceded. "Owen didn't land you in here."

"Didn't he? None of this would have happened if he'd stayed put yesterday as I ordered him to do. Isn't that right, Owen?"

"Yes," I said.

"You come all the way over here with some grandiose idea of rescuing me, and then your compulsive detective playing is the very thing that lands me in the soup."

I'd had so much experience at being browbeaten that it seldom took up my full attention. At that moment, I had enough left over to reflect on the words Swickard had chosen to describe his dilemma. "In the soup" seemed almost comically inadequate to me. One of the things you gave up for the religious life, I decided, was the kind of language you badly needed at a moment like this.

"We've come to discuss getting you out of here," Praed said. "Let's concentrate on that."

"How do you suggest we accomplish that miracle?" Swickard demanded of the major. Praed passed the question to me with a glance.

"Start by telling us your version of what happened last night," I said.

As he collected his thoughts, the priest ran his fingers through his long hair, tucking and retucking it behind his ears.

"I got back from visiting my sick parishioner later than I expected. Just before dinnertime. Of course I found you and Basil gone and no note to let me know where you'd run off to."

He paused then for his overdue explanation. I told him

of our fruitless walk to Somolet and of our encounter with Tot on the trip back.

"I know him," Swickard said. "A vagabond I've seen in about every corner of the valley."

"Would you have taken his word about having seen the sword?" Praed asked.

"I might have," Swickard said. "It's the kind of thing he would know. He pokes his nose in every farmhouse he comes to, looking for a handout."

That concession softened him somewhat. He invited us to sit down on the narrow bed, the only furniture in the cell besides the stool he was occupying. And when he told me to go on with my story, it was more a request than an order. I described the long trek to the Ngatini farm and what we'd found there.

"Just the kind of mistake you'd expect someone like Tot to make," the priest muttered.

He went on then with his own story. "I waited until it began to get dark. Then I called around to everyone I could think of whose line was working."

"Including Mwarai?" I asked.

"I tried to reach him. He was out. I wanted to send his men out looking for you. Instead I had to call Norris here and Rex Brocious back and ask them to help me. I asked the doctor to search around the village and the major to take the area east of it. I went west, along the river. I found no trace of you, of course.

"I returned to the mission a little before eight, intending to try the chief constable again. I found Wauki dead on the front steps. It was ghastly. This time Mwarai was in when I phoned. He and his men showed up less than ten minutes later."

"Him and his whole troop?" Praed asked. "That was fast

work."

"It got faster still. A minute after he arrived, the chief constable was placing me in custody. I'm afraid I reacted badly to that. I had a great deal of pent-up nervousness and anger, which I should have saved for you, Owen. Instead, I vented it on Chief Constable Mwarai. It ended with me being taken away, under guard, to spend the night in this cell."

It was a very clean cell, like the rest of Mwarai's domain. But it was still a cell. Between the time Praed called for the guard and the time the guard showed up, I had a chance to feel a little of the claustrophobia that Swickard must have been experiencing. I forgave him for his earlier name calling. That was premature, as it turned out.

The priest used those few moments to ask us what we intended to do next. Praed said, "Talk to Mwarai about getting you out of here. He's had a night to sleep on it; maybe he's come to his senses. And I have to tell him I sent Lori away."

I heard the jailer's footsteps approaching and remembered a question I wanted to put to the priest.

"How do I find Mugo?"

That brought the blood rushing back into Swickard's sunken temples. "How do you find Mugo? How do you find a bird you saw in a tree a month ago or a cloud you saw yesterday? Do you think he has an address? Do you suppose you can look him up in the phone book under mystics?"

As the constable unlocked the cell door, the priest turned to the major, "You should have sent this idiot away, too. Promise me you will if things go badly for me."

"He's safe with me," Praed said. Neither man addressed me. Not until the major and I were standing in Mwarai's anteroom. Even then Praed diplomatically avoided the subject of that last blowup, asking, "Was that right, what the padre said? About you coming over here because you had some kind of forewarning that he would be in trouble? What did you get, a premonition? A dream?"

"A draft notice," I said.

"Fancy him wanting to send you away though." He rubbed his nub of a chin thoughtfully. "I hope that's not a bad sign."

"How?" I asked.

"Like maybe he wants trouble. He says he mouthed off to Mwarai because he was mad at you, but maybe he deliberately provoked the chief constable. Maybe he's trying to make himself a martyr so the world will notice what's going on out here."

If Swickard was counting on the timid Director McKenzie to spread the word of his martyrdom, he was miscalculating. It was so large a miscalculation, in fact, that I couldn't imagine the priest making it. Someone else might have, though. Someone who'd never met McKenzie. Someone who was dying for a little excitement.

"Maybe whoever set Father Phil up was volunteering him for martyrdom," I said. "Maybe so the world will notice what's going on out here. Maybe just to raise a little hell."

I tried to shake Praed with an accusing look. He responded with a sardonic grin.

"If you think that's so," he said, "you should be asking yourself a question: If one martyr's good, would two be better?"

# CHAPTER FOURTEEN

The chief constable admitted us then. Praed had spoken of Mwarai's having had a night to sleep on things, but it looked to me as though the policeman had slept as badly as I had.

"Gentlemen," he said from behind his small and orderly desk. "What can I do for you this morning? I told you last night that I would call upon you if I needed you."

Praed led off with his excuse for our visit. "I wanted to tell you that Lori's driving our guests over to the Maasai Mara right about now. I told her she could stay on there for a few days. I thought you should know, in light of things."

Mwarai waved a hand at the news, using the little back-and-forth movement of the wrist favored by royalty. "Perfectly all right, I'm sure," he said with no interest at all. "Was there anything else?"

"Yes," Praed said. "Have there been any demonstrations by Wauki's followers?"

"None. The mission has been unmolested. His followers — so-called — appear to have scattered completely."

That fit with what Lori Praed had said about Wauki having no more true believers than he could afford to keep drunk.

"My men have been attempting to discover where Wauki slept most recently. It was his habit to move about. I am hoping to recover some personal items. So far they have reported no luck. It is as though even his former hosts do not wish to be associated with his memory."

"Since there've been no disturbances," Praed said, "We'd

like you to reconsider Father Swickard's protective custody. He'd be welcome to stay with me at the lodge. I'd be responsible for him. You could call it house arrest, if you like."

Mwarai's eyes were even more reddened than usual. They moved between Praed and me for a time as though we might be passing signals. Then he said, "Gentlemen, I'm afraid the situation has grown graver for Father Swickard. Come with me, please."

He led us next door to a room that might have been the Somolet crime lab. It held a whitewashed workbench on which was spread a short-sleeved white dress shirt stained across the front with dried blood. The stain ran diagonally, like the leather shoulder strap of Mwarai's uniform belt. There were lesser stains above and below it and on the sleeves.

Mwarai said, "This was found early this morning. It was caught on a thorn bush beneath one of the bluffs overlooking the river not far from the mission. Someone threw it from the height expecting it to be carried away by the current, but it caught on the bush. It has been positively identified as one of the priest's shirts by Etta, the woman who keeps his house."

To his credit, Mwarai didn't sound happy about it. He continued to look glum as he asked me, "Was Father Swickard wearing a shirt like this one when you saw him yesterday?"

"He's still wearing a shirt like this one," I said. "It's all he's worn since I got here, except for the night of Miss Chesney's party, when he wore his clericals."

"Then he would naturally have changed into a similar shirt when he returned last night from the river," the policeman said.

"After washing himself," I said.

"Yes," Mwarai said.

"Tell me then, Chief Constable. Why did he throw the shirt from the top of the bluff?"

"As I said, so the river would carry it away."

"But he was going to the river itself, in your scenario. To wash. Why wouldn't he have just carried the shirt down to the water with him? He could have thrown it in then or sunk it with a rock or fed it to the crocodiles. Whoever threw that shirt from the bluff wanted it to be found, so it would implicate Father Swickard."

"You're suggesting that the murderer wore a shirt of the priest's during the commission of the crime?"

"Yes, knowing a lot of blood would be tossed around."

"And how did this person obtain the shirt?"

"From the clothesline at the mission. Etta had the laundry out and drying when I left yesterday. Didn't she mention that? Anyone could have come by and taken a shirt."

"I've seen laundry there often myself," Praed contributed.

"This someone stole the shirt without Etta noticing? Without the children noticing? No, gentlemen. Father Swickard threw the shirt from the bluff. What seems illogical to you seemed very logical to him last night. Look at it, stained with another man's blood. Not the blood of Christ either, of which the priest speaks so often. Not wine magically transformed into blood. Just blood. He would have taken it off as soon as he could, just as he did with the gloves. He would have thrown it away at the first possible moment. That is why he did not wait until he had climbed down to the river itself."

Mwarai had invited us to look at the shirt again, so I did. And I belatedly noticed that, while the diagonal stain on the shirt's right front met the diagonal stain on the shirt's left front, the buttons didn't align with the button holes. That is, someone had arranged the shirt so as to make sense of the stain, without regard for whether or not the shirt would button.

I asked for permission to touch the shirt and then tugged at the stiff cloth until the buttons lined up with the holes. Now the diagonal stain formed a zigzag, like a cartoon lightning bolt, instead of a continuous line.

"Well I'll be damned," Praed said. "How did the blood jog like that?"

"It didn't," I said. "It splashed the shirt in one go, probably when the death blow was struck. The two sides don't line up because the shirt wasn't buttoned when it happened. Has anyone ever seen Father Swickard in an unbuttoned shirt?"

"Never," Praed said. "Nor even an unpressed one. Lori and I've often joked about it. He dresses like he's always expecting the Pope. And he doesn't wear a shirt untucked either. But look, there's a little blood down on the very bottom."

"I have never seen his shirt hanging open either," Mwarai admitted. "Or untucked. But it might have become disarranged in the struggle."

"There was no struggle," I said. "Wauki was taken by surprise and killed by a single blow."

"That is true," the policeman said.

I followed up my momentary advantage. "A larger man wearing Father Swickard's shirt would have to have left it unbuttoned."

"Just about any man would have," Praed said. "The padre's no weight lifter."

The chief constable's confidence was shaken. In an effort to regroup, he said, "There are still questions to be answered. Why did Wauki come to the mission last night? The deadline for the return of the sword was not until the day after the full moon, which is tomorrow. And how did Father Swickard—or whoever did the killing—know that Wauki would be there?"

I noted with approval Mwarai's concession about the murderer's identity. And the suggestion that he was still willing to speculate, however grudgingly.

"While we're listing unanswered questions," I said, "we

should discuss the killer's motive. It has to somehow involve the land scandal. Both Father Swickard and Wauki spoke out against that. Now both men are silenced, one dead and the other in jail. We've got to look into the land business if we want to learn the truth."

"Give it up, Owen," Praed said. "The chief constable is never going to follow that trail. He knows it will lead him right back to his own bosses."

Praed was trying to help the cause by prodding Mwarai. I spotted that, and I assumed Mwarai had, too. But for a moment, I thought the major had overplayed it.

Mwarai turned back to the bloody shirt, pulling the two sides of the front apart but keeping the buttons level with the holes. When the stains aligned again, the shirt was open a full six inches.

Speaking slowly, the policeman said, "As a matter of fact, I have received a summons this morning from the chief of the Nihuru. He wishes to speak with me on the subject of land theft. I had intended to send my apologies, given last night's events. But to prove my good faith to you, I will go. If you wish, Mr. Keane, you may accompany me."

## CHAPTER FIFTEEN

Mwarai hadn't included Major Praed in his invitation to visit the chief of the Nihuru. I was expecting the aggressive major to invite himself, but that didn't happen. Praed explained his sudden shyness to me while we stood in the dirt street in front of the police station, waiting for Mwarai to appear. As he talked, the soldier creased and recreased the crown of his Jungle Jim hat, which was the twin of one I'd turned down in Nairobi.

"You might do better if I'm not along, Owen. You may not have noticed, but I tend to chafe the chief constable just a mite."

"I've noticed," I said.

"He likes you, though. Especially in comparison to me. That might work in our favor."

"Good cop, bad cop," I said. I thought I'd have to explain the reference to Praed, but he was familiar with it. He might have been another fan of American detective shows, like Noah the bush pilot.

"Bingo," he said. "Using the technique against the police is a trifle unusual, but turnabout is fair play. I'll keep being a horse's ass, and you keep being his best mate. Between us, we may nudge him toward the light."

He drew me a step closer to the center of the street. We weren't running much of a risk. The only traffic I'd seen so far was a man pulling a cart configured like a ricksha, but with wheels from an old jeep.

Praed said, "A word in your ear about Chief Joseph Wamba. He could be exactly what we need: another suspect. Wauki was as big a nuisance to Wamba as he ever was to the padre. If you can get Mwarai mulling over the chief's motives, he may loosen up on Father Phil. But it's a potentially dangerous card for you to play."

"Why?"

"Wamba's a sly old bird. You don't get to be a tribal chief if you're not. And he isn't just a figurehead. The way things work here in Kenya, the chiefs wield a lot of power. That's yet another hedge against true democracy maintained by the powers that be in Nairobi. Bright bureaucrats like Karari Gathitu may be slowly taking over, but the old tribal structure is still strong. I think Gathitu would win a tug-of-war with Wamba if it ever came to that, but it would be a close-run thing."

"How big a threat was Wauki to Wamba?"

Praed had given up creasing his hat and was using it to chase some flies away. "A deadly threat, in theory. I mean, if enough of the Nihuru had taken Wauki's claims seriously, he could have challenged Wamba for leadership of the tribe. That hadn't happened, not that I could see. Now it never will happen."

Which gave Wamba a motive for Wauki's murder, at least on paper. But it didn't give him a very compelling reason for framing Swickard so elaborately. Not unless Wamba was involved in the land scandal himself or wanted the publicity Swickard's martyrdom might give the little valley. I decided I'd have to wait to meet the chief before I'd know whether to play Praed's dangerous card.

I lost the Australian's company and counsel at that point, but picked up Basil's. He came trotting down the main street just as the major marched off and the chief constable pulled around the municipal building in his official jeep.

"What are you doing here, little one?" Mwarai asked the boy.

Basil answered at length, but not in English. Mwarai interpreted for me.

"He finds the farm of the cook's brother boring. He'd rather investigate crimes with you, but I think he's embarrassed to ask. He's afraid he let you down last night."

Basil certainly acted embarrassed. Throughout Mwarai's translation, he drew in the dust with the open toe of his shoe. For him, it was a major emotional display.

"If you'd like to bring him along," the policeman said, "I've no objections."

"I would," I said.

Basil was climbing into the jeep before I could add any words of absolution regarding the previous evening, his contrition well under control. I took the seat beside Mwarai.

We drove north out of Somolet, heading away from the mission. The road meandered around a series of wooded hills before returning to farmland.

Unlike Philip Swickard, Mwarai could drive and talk at the same time. Drive and cross-examine.

"What was the major telling you just now so earnestly?" he asked me.

"About Joseph Wamba. He said he wasn't just a figurehead."

"By no means. He's another of my superiors. I find some days that I have nothing but superiors. Real ones and self-appointed ones like the major. Are you satisfied with his explanation of his movements last evening?"

"Major Praed's? It would be a difficult story to check."

"Exactly. He drives around searching for you without success. Very difficult to verify. And when he really wants to find you, he drives right to you."

Praed had said that we needed other suspects. I couldn't wait to tell him who Mwarai had tapped for the role.

"What would his motive be?"

"A man with a beautiful wife always has a motive," Mwarai said. "I have not been able to discover much about Wauki, but I have learned that he had what they call an eye for the ladies."

I'd heard something along the same lines, from Lorelei Praed no less. And I'd observed firsthand Praed's dour reaction to his wife's outgoing nature. As for the major's motive for framing Swickard, he'd told me himself that Lori enjoyed flirting with the priest.

"What else did you learn about Wauki?"

"That he was educated, but not well educated. Self educated, like as not. That he'd done manual labor, but not recently, probably as a boy and a young man. That he'd probably spent time in prison."

Those bits of speculation sounded like deductions. What was more, they had a familiar ring. "Did Elizabeth Chesney come to those conclusions?"

"Yes," Mwarai said. He seemed slightly embarrassed that I'd identified the source of his information. "She is a very … insightful person. I have come to trust her judgment of people."

Including, I suspected, her judgment of me, his "best mate." I risked a little of my favored status then. "Would you mind my asking about your movements yesterday, Chief Constable?"

Mwarai stiffened beside me. "Are you another of my superiors?"

"Just a man trying to be thorough."

"I see. As a good investigator you are naturally thorough."

"Basil and I stopped by to see you yesterday afternoon, but you were gone. And Father Swickard tried to reach you before he set out to look for me. He was told you hadn't returned."

"Quite true. I went up valley yesterday to have a scout around. I'd heard a rumor of some trouble." He downshifted us through a tight bend in the road before adding, "Poachers."

"Didn't you say the other night that the valley doesn't have poachers?"

"And I intend to keep it that way. In any case, we found nothing."

"Father Swickard said you responded very quickly and in force when he reported the murder."

"Again, the explanation is simple. I had sent out several scouting patrols yesterday. As it happened, I was hearing their reports when the priest's call came in. Does that answer satisfy you?"

"Yes," I said.

"I am pleased. Now we can go forward as colleagues."

I was pleased with that myself. I asked about our destination and Mwarai referred me to a map in the jeep's doorless glove compartment. Basil took an interest in this document, resting his head on my shoulder so he could study it closely.

It was the first map of the Nihuru Valley I'd seen. At Chesney's party, Major Praed had described the valley as a cleft in the true escarpment. The map showed the cleft to be roughly the shape of an arrowhead, though a better image was a leaf, with the Nihuru River as the stem and its tributary creeks the veins.

"We are going to the village of Agat," the policeman said. "Ten kilometers north of Somolet."

I found it on the map, but only a moment or two before the real thing appeared in the road before us.

"Agat," Mwarai announced. "Ancestral seat of the chiefs of the Nihuru."

## CHAPTER SIXTEEN

Agat was the first place I'd seen in Kenya that had been built to a master plan. That plan evidently called for long frame buildings almost the size of army barracks, with board and batten siding painted white and tin roofs painted gray. These were set on shaded lots separated by what were either very broad paths or very narrow streets. One building stood out from the others due to its central location and a front porch as wide as the structure and almost as deep. On that porch sat Chief Joseph Wamba.

Basil and I were presented to him rather than introduced. He didn't rise from his chair for the ceremony, but that would have been a considerable and perhaps painful effort. Wamba was a large man gone to fat, and his legs and ankles appeared to be badly swollen. He was gray-bearded and gray-haired, and each of his ear lobes was stretched by a massive golden ring. The tops of his ears were also under pressure: bent outward by the arms of glasses thicker even than those of Dr. Brocious and of the same unstylish Buddy Holly design. He was missing teeth, but nothing like the majority. He wore a homespun shirt similar in design to the one Karari Gathitu had worn to the party but more richly colored, in reds and greens. His pants were roughly cut off at the knee, displaying his distended legs. His large hands rested on the head of a shillelagh-like stick nearly as big around as the supports of the porch roof.

I decided that if Wamba had killed Wauki he'd hired it

out. There was no shortage of labor in the village, male and female both. Our arrival had actually drawn a crowd.

The chief extended his welcome and his offer of food and drink through Mwarai, who stood at attention with his royal blue uniform cap under one arm. The policeman explained to me that Wamba didn't think his English was up to the occasion. But when the chief noticed me returning the curious stares of the onlookers, he plunged in in a raspy voice.

"You like my people, Owen Keane?"

"Yes," I said.

"They like you think?"

I begged his pardon.

"As you expected," Mwarai said.

Wamba nodded. "Expected. You expected them naked? You expected them covered with mud and feathers?"

"No," I said.

Wamba wasn't buying. "Other chiefs show their people that way." He asked Mwarai for a word.

"Tourists," the policeman supplied.

"To tourists. For one shilling, two shillings, the chiefs let the tourists enter the huts, sit on the dirt, smell the cook fire. I do not. Tourist people want me to. I do not. Nihuru do not live in the dirt for tourist shillings. We do not live in the past for tourists."

"Mr. Keane is not a tourist," Mwarai assured him. "He is a friend of your friend, Philip Swickard. He is trying to help his friend."

"I hear of Philip's trouble. I mourn for the little man. I do not mourn for Wauki. He spoke lies. He. . ."

Wamba's English, which had loosened up wonderfully, failed him then. He spoke passionately to Mwarai for a time. The policeman summarized for me.

"Wauki called Chief Wamba a tool of the Nairobi gov-

118

ernment. He accused him of secretly being in the pay of the government."

It was the very charge Wauki had leveled against Swickard, except that the murdered man had specifically tied the priest to the land scandal. I started to ask Mwarai if he'd omitted that detail from his summary of Wamba's lament. I decided I'd ask the chief directly.

"Did Wauki accuse you of being part of a scheme to steal land from your people?"

Wamba brought his heavy stick down on the plank floor of the porch with a thump. "The lie! Wauki's lie! He said I help those who want to prey on my people! That I kiss their hands!"

If he'd worked a little spittle into it, he would have matched Swickard's reaction perfectly. Wamba's variation was to thump his cane twice more in anger.

Mwarai said, "You sent word that you have news of land thieves. I've come to speak to you about that."

Wamba nodded solemnly. "It has begun, Samuel. As I warned you. As the little priest warned you. To the valley of the Nihuru, it has come."

He surprised me then by rising to his feet in one swift determined motion. His next movements were slower, but no less resolute. When he neared the stairs where we stood, he handed his cudgel to Basil. He put one hand on my shoulder and the other on Mwarai's, and we descended the stairs together. We walked three abreast through the small crowd of silent onlookers, Basil preceding us with the walking stick like an acolyte with his candle. At a slow march we crossed Agat's town square to a building without a porch but with many screened windows and wide screened doors. These were opened as we approached. Wamba climbed the building's three steps even more deliberately, transmitting to me a little of the pain he was in by squeezing my shoulder.

The building was set up as a dispensary, with a row of cots along one wall, some in the part of the room we occupied, some beyond a curtain divider. Half a dozen of the cots on our side of the curtain were in use. While the only sources of light were the well-shaded windows, I could see that most of the patients were bandaged.

Mwarai and Wamba conversed in low, hospital-room tones. The chief had switched back to his stick, freeing me to move about, hat in hand. I walked from cot to cot, forcing a smile that became progressively more wooden. The cots contained four boys and two men. Beyond the much patched white curtain were other cots containing women and girls and small children. A nurse blocked my entry to that sanctum. I counted eight additional sufferers before she drew the curtain fully closed.

As far as I could tell, the worst injuries were on my end of the room. One man appeared to have lost the fingers of his right hand. His head was swathed in bandages that covered one ear, if the ear was still there. He and I exchanged long looks. I read pain and resignation in his half-closed eyes. God knows what he made of my, by then, manic smile.

Mwarai joined me. "These are the survivors of three *shambas* attacked and burned last night. These people had no more warning than their dogs could give them. The attackers used machetes and automatic weapons. Three men were killed trying to resist. The rest were driven into the bush."

"Who were these attackers?" I asked.

"They don't know. Strangers, on foot. Our valley is very close to the border. It might have been bandits who slipped across and have already gone back."

"Bandits?" Wamba rasped. He'd been given a stool to sit on, which made his cane available for some floor thumping that started a child crying in the space beyond the curtain. "Bandits? My people have nothing to steal except their land. The strangers were land bandits, land. . ."

This time he looked to me for the right word. "Raiders," I said.

"Land raiders," Wamba repeated, pounding the floor again. "They frighten people off their land. Kill them off their land. I told you this was coming. The priest told you. Even the fool Wauki told you. What will you do, Samuel?"

Mwarai did what he did best: maintained his dignity. He questioned the injured men and then the women, getting short, grudging, frightened answers that he didn't bother to translate. That didn't worry me. Basil was dogging his heels, missing nothing.

After a tense half hour, Mwarai gave it up. "I must go back and make my report," he said. "I will need additional men. And perhaps an airplane to track these. . . raiders. But they are probably already across the border."

"They are sleeping now, like the lion," Wamba said. "Soon they will stalk their next *shamba*, like the lion stalks its dinner."

"I will send Dr. Brocious out to help your nurse."

The chief actually said "bah" to that. "I will take care of my people. What can the doctor do that we haven't done? Next you will send Mugo to shake feathers at them and chant."

"Mugo the mystic?" I asked.

"Yes," Wamba said. "Another fakir, like the dead Wauki. Another troublemaker. You know Mugo, Owen Keane?"

"Father Swickard told me about him. I think he might be Father Swickard's enemy."

"He is the enemy of all modern men."

"Do you know where we can find him?"

"His camp is in the forest, beyond the river. Far to the

south." Then Wamba added as an afterthought, "Yesterday he was here."

Mwarai took an interest in that. "Mugo was in Agat yesterday?"

"And in Somolet last night," Wamba said. "Many have told me. Did no one tell you, Samuel?"

"No," the policeman said.

"You must talk to the people always, Samuel."

"Mugo could have been at the mission last night when Wauki was killed," I said.

Mwarai shrugged and asked the chief, "What did he want?"

"To make trouble. He wants the Nihuru to live in the dirt. To wear mud and animal skins."

"Who is he?" I asked.

This time Wamba shrugged, putting far more into it than the policeman had. "A man of the forest. The dead Wauki was a man of the city. Our valley is not forest and it is not city."

I wanted to hear more of this urban Wauki, but Mwarai was very suddenly and very obviously anxious to take me away.

"I must make my report," he said again.

Wamba saw us as far as the dispensary's double door. "*Kwaheri*, Owen Keane. Tell Philip that he was right. That must be his comfort now. He was a good friend to the Nihuru."

# CHAPTER SEVENTEEN

Chief Wamba's use of the past tense to describe Swickard wasn't lost on me. I started in on the chief constable as soon as we were back in the jeep.

"Quite a coincidence, those raids taking place last night. The very night Wauki was murdered."

"Of course you mean that it is no coincidence," Mwarai said, "that as an investigator you are trained to distrust coincidence. And yet coincidence is a part of life."

It was an observation Elizabeth Chesney might have made playfully or Rex Brocious philosophically or Norris Praed cynically. Mwarai said it resignedly. His attitude reminded me of the look I'd seen in the eyes of the wounded man in Wamba's little hospital. Something bad had happened. More bad was sure to follow. The cautious policeman was seeing trouble for himself everywhere he looked.

"Do you think it was a coincidence?" I asked. No answer. "Do you think Mugo's being in the neighborhood last night was a coincidence?"

"What do you think, Mr. Keane?"

I was actually thinking of Major Praed's observation that we needed other suspects to draw Mwarai's attention away from Swickard. Praed had looked for Joseph Wamba to provide that distraction, but I preferred the mystic who had somehow foreseen my arrival in Kenya.

"What do you know about Mugo?" I asked.

"Almost nothing. He breaks no laws, nor does he make

123

himself available to be questioned."

"I was told that he's behind the disappearance of Father Swickard's assistant, Daniel."

"Were you told that Mugo kidnapped the boy?"

"No, that Daniel ran off to join him."

"Then it is no business of mine. Who told you of this?"

"The boy's aunt, the cook, Ruth."

Mwarai grunted. "One of the people Chief Joseph thinks I should be speaking to. But do they speak to me? No. This uniform does not make it easier to speak to my own people. It makes it much harder."

I would have made some soothing reply about the policeman's lot, but I noticed just then that we were no longer on the winding road to Somolet.

"I must see the doctor," Mwarai explained. "To tell him of the situation in Agat and to get his report on Wauki. His clinic is almost on our way. Just a little to the west."

Dr. Brocious's clinic might have been another former great house, like the mission. It was as large as Swickard's house, but more rambling, and its walls were stucco rather than stone. White stucco that hadn't been painted recently and had been patched here and there with a rough gray material, maybe cement, maybe mud. It gave the house a blotchy look that wasn't reassuring in a medical facility.

That hadn't kept the patients away. The waiting room—the old building's flagged front porch—was fairly full. I noticed Mwarai scanning the crowd and realized that he was looking for burns and machete wounds. I looked then, too, but saw none.

Brocious received us in his study. Two of us only, Basil having been delegated to guard the jeep by the chief constable, who told me, "He's heard quite enough of violence and blood for one morning." The study was incredibly dusty and jammed with books. I only had a second to glance at them, but it struck me that the doctor was a man who valued books for their content, not as physical objects. The bulk of his library was unlovely paperbacks and battered hardcovers.

As usual, Brocious was dressed for a cricket match, one called on account of rain in 1958, if I had to guess. But he was less red-faced and sweaty than on our previous meetings.

Mwarai began by telling him of the victims we'd just seen at the Agat dispensary. He said that he'd offered to send Brocious out there but didn't mention Chief Wamba's dismissal of the idea. He didn't have to mention it.

"I expect his highness failed to jump at that offer," Brocious said, removing his glasses and passing a hand over his pliant features. "One self-sufficient old bugger is Joseph Wamba. If *he* ever starts claiming to be the reincarnation of old Wauki, I'll be half inclined to believe it."

That brought us to the subject of the most recent claimant to the title. Brocious shuffled papers on his desk without appearing to ever find what he was looking for. Then he said, "In the best traditions of the medical examiners in every mystery story I ever read, I'm sticking to the snap judgments I made last night. Time of death, sunset, give or take an hour. Cause of death, the first blow of that old vengeance weapon, the cutlass. Subsequent blows purely gratuitous. Not even done to disguise the identity of the victim, as in a decent whodunit, since the face was untouched."

Brocious lit a cigarette, offered me one, and when I turned him down said, "Back on your feet, eh? Good man."

"What have you learned of the victim himself?" Mwarai asked.

"Precious little. There were no obvious marks of reincarnation, not that I have the slightest notion of what those marks might be. On the other hand, there were some indications that he'd lived a considerable portion of his life in a city."

Mwarai stirred a little at that confirmation of Wamba's insight, but he said nothing.

I asked, "What indications?"

"Dental work mostly. A better grade than you'll get from our roving practitioners here in the wild. Some older examples and some newer ones, hence the surmise that he lived in the city or at least visited one regularly over some span of time."

"Nairobi?" I asked.

"Or London or Pittsburgh. I've no way of knowing."

"Anything else?" the policeman asked.

"Some scarring around the brows and on the knuckles of the hands that suggests he wasn't always a man of peace. And from the look of his liver, he liked his daily tot. Not that I hold drinking against any soul, reincarnated or not.

"Speaking of which, can I offer you something, Owen? The chief constable isn't a drinking man, but he tolerates the weakness in others."

"A little early for me," I said.

Brocious's professional eye may have told him that I'd bent that rule regularly in the past few months, but he didn't call me on it. He pushed his sliding glasses back into place and said, "Then I'd best sort through my patients and get myself out to Agat."

"Thank you, Doctor," Mwarai said, rising.

"And I'll see to Wauki's burial, shall I? We can't put that off much longer. You can always dig him up again, if some question arises as to whether he's remained dead."

Mwarai's smudge of a moustache twitched. "Of course," he said.

"Perhaps I'll ask Chief Wamba to say a few words at the service," the doctor added, grinning.

"I will send you the internment order," the unsmiling

policeman replied as he turned on his heel.

I hurried to follow him out.

## CHAPTER EIGHTEEN

None of us spoke as we drove away from the clinic. I was thinking of Wauki the city man, trying to see a way that tiny bit of biography might help, might explain his murder, might have threatened someone or been a threat to Wauki himself in the wrong hands. I couldn't. If you believed Wauki's spirit could live again, you wouldn't balk at its choosing an urban birth. If you didn't believe in reincarnation, the details of an individual's background wouldn't make you believe any less.

By then we were driving through a patch of forest. Mwarai hadn't taken us back to the main road. The track we were on was only a little wider than the jeep. I decided it must be a shortcut to Somolet. It certainly fit my general experience of shortcuts, which was that they're hard on both shock absorbers and patience.

When Mwarai finally spoke, I realized that his preceding silence had stemmed from a renewed sense of grievance.

"The doctor is not a respectful man. He does not respect individuals or ranks or situations. I know this is the result of him not respecting himself. Still, it makes him very unpleasant to work with."

Basil suddenly placed a hand on the policeman's shoulder. The movement was so swift and firm that I didn't have a chance to mistake it for a sympathetic act. Neither did Mwarai. He was braking the jeep even before Basil shouted, "Stop!"

As we slid to a halt, the trees to our left began to sway madly, as though they'd been hit by a very localized tornado.

Or rather an earthquake, one that became less localized by the second. The rhythmic pounding made the jeep's cheap dashboard vibrate like a sounding board. Then the trees parted and an elephant strode onto the road.

I'd probably seen a dozen living elephants in my lifetime, in parades and circuses and zoos, and hundreds more filmed ones on television. None of those exposures prepared me for the size of this animal at the range of a car length. Or the easy speed at which it moved. I had time to note its tusks and the surprising shape of its conical skull with its deeply sunken temples. Then it was into the woods on the other side of the road. A second elephant appeared, the size of the first, then one half that size, and finally a baby, so small that Basil had to stand in his seat to get a view unobstructed by the windscreen.

After they'd passed, we sat on for a time like people who had been narrowly missed by a freight train at a faulty crossing. Then Mwarai said, "That is our current situation, Mr. Keane. It can turn that dangerous that quickly and with that little warning. And I once wished for an American-style murder case. I could bite my tongue."

He got us rolling again and asked, "In your opinion, what would a proper next move be?"

To give me time to think, I said, "Tell me more about Mugo. When did he come to this area?"

"Some believe he has always been here, like the valley itself. I first heard of him perhaps a year ago."

"Another newcomer then," I said. "Like Wauki."

"You might as easily say, 'Like the Praeds.' And what of it? The trouble with not believing in coincidence, Mr. Keane, is that you end up believing instead in connections that do not exist, in hidden forces and secret patterns. You end by seeking a single explanation for everything. No such explanation exists."

Now you tell me, I thought. I said, "I think the proper next move would be a talk with Mugo."

He gave the idea a winding mile's thought, but ended up tossing it back. "The situation in Agat must be dealt with first. Everything else must take second place, even Wauki's murder."

"Even Philip Swickard," I said, hoping to make him re-examine his priorities, but he merely nodded in agreement.

By then we were roaring into Somolet. The town should have been in the midst of its midday siesta, but an arrival prior to ours had perked things up. A dark blue Toyota Land Cruiser, miraculously free of dust, was parked in front of the police station. The Kenyan flag hung limply from a miniature staff attached to its hood.

"Commissioner Gathitu has returned early from his trip," Mwarai said, his dead tone reminding me of the warning of sudden danger he'd drawn from the mini elephant stampede.

I'd mentally discarded the government man, since I'd thought him safely tucked away in Nairobi. I should have been expecting him to react in some way to the news of Wauki's death. Even then I didn't see his return as a truly bad omen. Not until we were out of the jeep and I spotted a hesitation amounting to dread in Mwarai. Basil's contribution to our collective mood was a flat refusal to accompany us into the station.

Gathitu was in the chief constable's little office, though it would be more correct to say he had taken it over. He sat behind the desk, speaking on the telephone, resplendent today in a cap and vest of a black cloth brocaded in a golden thread that very nearly matched the frames of his sunglasses. He acknowledged our arrival only by raising a hand to hold us in the doorway.

I'd heard him say "Yes" several times and "We will

discuss it in person" while Mwarai and I were crossing the anteroom. He dropped English as soon as I appeared in the doorway, only to return to it shortly afterward when he lost his connection.

"Hello? Hello? Damn this service." He slammed down the handset. "Come in, Chief Constable. I've been awaiting your report. Your long overdue report. The telephone message you left for me this morning was far from adequate. We will discuss that presently. In the meantime, I must congratulate you on the prompt resolution of this terrible business. I only regret that I was forced to learn of your success by questioning your subordinates due to your absence from your post."

"I, I did not expect you to return this morning," the policeman stammered.

"Obviously. However, you have done the most important thing. You have apprehended the murderer. Congratulations on that excellent work."

"My investigation is incomplete."

Gathitu began to tap the desktop impatiently. "No doubt there are minor points to be resolved." I was surprised to find that I came under that heading. "Is this man in your custody?"

"Mr. Keane? No. He has been assisting me in my investigation."

"Assisting you?" Gathitu sprang to his feet, sending Mwarai to full attention. "This friend of the murderer? Assisting you how? By filling your head with doubts? Are we so backward in Somolet that we need Americans to do our thinking for us? And what do we know of this American, this famous detective? The American consul in Nairobi has never heard of him. What are his credentials? You take the word of an old woman and a priest and promote this man over your own head. I am seriously displeased with you, Chief Constable."

Of the deference I'd received from the commissioner at Elizabeth Chesney's, there was no sign. In fact, Gathitu had yet to address me or turn his head my way. His cold manner was a clear warning, but I ignored it, shouldering my way past the silent Mwarai.

"Three farms were attacked last night north of Agat," I said.

"And how is that your business?" Gathitu demanded.

Mwarai stepped between us again. "We believe the attacks and the murder of the man who called himself Wauki may be connected."

"*We* believe?" Gathitu's light voice became shrill. "You mean this American tourist believes it and you are following him like his pet dog. Those attacks, as you call them, were probably random acts of mischief committed by poachers. As such, they can be handled by the government's anti-poaching unit. That is why the unit was created. They are no concern of yours, Chief Constable, and certainly no concern of your American advisor. They can have no bearing on your investigation, do you understand? You have your murderer. Resolve any minor difficulties you may have and write your report. I will expect to receive it tomorrow at the very latest. Do I make myself clear?"

Mwarai all but clicked his heels. "Yes, sir!"

"As for you, Mr. Owen Keane, your high-handed behavior has cost you your welcome in this valley. Once I am satisfied that you were not an accomplice in this affair, you will be returned to Nairobi. You are staying where?"

The policeman answered for me. "The Somolet Lodge."

"Return there and await my instructions."

Mwarai pivoted to face me. "I will arrange for you to be driven over."

"You will do no such thing, Chief Constable. Mr. Keane has enjoyed quite enough of your largesse. He can walk."

## CHAPTER NINETEEN

Basil was waiting for me by the jeep.

"Bad news," I said. "You have to go back to Ruth's brother's farm. In fact, I'm going to take you there myself."

He absorbed the bad news and the good news with equal stoicism, only raising his eyebrows toward his widow's peak when I reached into the jeep's cubbyhole glove compartment and extracted Mwarai's map of the valley. If the policeman didn't know his way around by now, he never would.

"Lead the way," I said.

The way took us so close to Elizabeth Chesney's cottage that I ordered a detour. Leaving Basil to patrol the bee perimeter, I knocked on the blue cottage's front door. The only answer was a deep barking that sounded as though it was coming from behind the house. I followed a stone path around to the back, thinking that Chesney might be working in her garden. She was there, but she wasn't puttering. She was seated in a camp chair, staring out toward the green hills. Reggie was seated beside her, staring at me and growling softly.

Without shifting her focus to me, Chesney said, "Reggie has already identified you as a friend."

Which he was demonstrating by not taking off my arm, presumably.

"A terrible business," the old woman said, repeating the very words Gathitu had used but sounding as though she meant them. "Norris Praed stopped by to bring me up to date.

133

I would have gone to the mission last night if I had known. Little good would that have done."

Chesney still wasn't looking at me. She appeared to be in a mild daze. From shock, I decided, wondering how often I'd appeared that way to people over the past two years.

She was dressed in blue again, this time a dress faded to the sun-bleached shade of her cottage. With it she wore a straw hat whose brim ended in a fat roll all the way around. It was a hat only a child or an old woman could carry off. In her spotted hands she held a single white rose.

I said, "Three other men died last night. There were farms attacked north of Agat. Chief Wamba thinks the attackers were land raiders."

That might not have been news to her either; I wasn't exactly sure. She didn't react as though it was. She didn't really react at all. Afraid I was driving her further into herself, I added, "Commissioner Gathitu thinks it was the work of poachers."

"He's back then," she said, rousing herself a little. And then, dismissively, "Poachers."

"What is the anti-poaching unit?"

"Why do you ask?"

"Gathitu thinks these attacks are the unit's problem. Who are they?"

"A group of ill-equipped, ill-trained soldiers sent out to track down the scum who murder elephants for their tusks and rhino for their horns. The idea was sound. The local police don't have the men or firepower to face down the poachers. But the anti-poaching unit is slow to react and far weaker than it appears to be on paper. God help them if they should actually encounter these raiders. It would be old Enfield rifles versus automatic weapons. The unit wouldn't stand a chance."

"Who would?" I asked.

"Who would?" she repeated and started to sag again.

To prop her up, I asked, "What can you tell me of Mugo?"

I'd actually come to ask her that, not to weigh her down with bad news. Mwarai trusted her judgment of people, and I trusted Mwarai's judgment. When he wasn't in the same room as Gathitu, anyway.

"Mugo?" She finally looked at me. "Why?"

"He may be someone who wished Philip Swickard no good. Chief Wamba called Mugo the enemy of all modern men."

"He must seem that way to Chief Joseph," Chesney said musingly. "And yet Mugo may be the most modern of us all. What characterizes the modern world more than a desire to turn back time to some dream of Arcadia? How else can you explain all the neo-paganism one reads about? Even on the unthinking, herd level one sees it, in the tattooing and the piercing so popular in your country and in Europe.

"Mugo is a Kenyan example of this general backward longing. He and his followers hope for a spiritual return to a pre-British, pre-Western time for this land. I suppose in a way our dead Wauki represented the same hope, but in a vague political sense."

"So Wauki and Mugo might have been rivals?"

"Or allies. I really couldn't say, Owen."

Reggie didn't like the first name stuff. He began growling at me again. Chesney pulled at his studded collar, and the dog stood up, backing me into the flora. "Go and stand guard with Basil," Chesney said to him. "He's there peeping over the butterfly bush. He'll scratch your ears for you. Go now." She didn't bother to watch him go. I did. He trotted straight to Basil and immediately presented ears.

"I must confess that I've never really met Mr. Mugo," Chesney was saying. "To be truthful, I've only seen him once. It was here in my garden. Rather, I was here. He was over there, by those trees. I hadn't heard him approach. Even Reggie hadn't. It's a specialty of Mugo's, the stealthy approach. He likes to simply appear, like a conjurer. There's a touch of vanity in that. And in the dress he affects. White robes are not particularly practical in this country."

"What did he do?"

"He stared at me. I had the impression that he'd been staring at me for some little while as I worked. I waited for him to come to me—at my age I expect that courtesy, even from holy men—but he never did. After a time he simply slipped back into the trees."

"So what was he doing?"

"Sizing up the enemy perhaps. I am, or was, a school teacher. After the soldiers and the missionaries, we were the major conduits of what I'm sure Mugo sees as Western contamination. I would have enjoyed discussing the point with him, if he'd given me the chance. Philip describes him as being very erudite.

"And I would like to have asked him what brought him to this valley. According to Philip, Mugo spoke of being drawn here by the valley's spiritual dissonance, whatever that might mean. Have you had any sense of that yourself, Owen?"

"Why would I have?" I asked, instantly defensive over whatever Swickard might have told her about me.

Chesney's hooded eyes were all innocence. "As another outsider, you might be aware of things we residents have grown too familiar with to notice."

"Are you sure Mugo is an outsider? Chief Constable Mwarai told me that Mugo's followers believe he's always been here."

"Did he? I very much doubt that the chief constable has spoken to even one of those followers. And any rumors he's heard are likely to be Mugo's own work.

"Mugo is not a Nihuru, Owen. I have Chief Joseph's own word for that. He is almost certainly a Kenyan, one educated in England, I suspect." She checked herself then. "Of course, my own little theories of Mugo are based on information passed to me by Father Philip. You could get this information firsthand from him."

"No, I can't." I decided not to tell her of the house-arrest order I was flaunting. Telling her might have involved her in my escape. "I tried to talk to him about Mugo this morning. He wasn't interested in the subject. I guess he couldn't understand what it has to do with Wauki's murder."

"I'm afraid I must agree with him there, Owen. I don't see what you're after. Major Praed indicated to me that you believe the land theft is ultimately behind the murder. Surely what you learned from Chief Wamba strengthened that view."

"According to Chief Wamba, Mugo was in the neighborhood yesterday. Out near Agat, where the attacks took place, and here in Somolet, where the murder occurred. If there's a link between the attacks and the murder, Mugo may be it."

Chesney reacted to that by closing her turtle eyes. She sat with them closed so long my attention wandered. When a shadow passed across the garden, I scanned the sky to find its source. I saw some kind of large bird circling between us and the still-high sun. One of Mugo's spies, I decided.

Presently Chesney completed her deliberations or just woke up from her nap. "I think Mugo is the line you should pursue, Owen. Do you have any idea how you'll proceed?"

"A vague one," I said. "But it might be better if you're not involved. I may need someone to post bail."

"You're right, of course. Still, I must help in some way."

She extended a hand to me, and I helped her from her chair. Reggie trotted back from his outpost, first to keep an eye on the chair extraction and then to bring up the rear as Chesney and I walked arm-in-arm to her French doors.

I was left alone on the patio where I'd shared a nightcap with Dr. Brocious. When Chesney returned, she was carrying the canteen I'd seen hanging in her trophy room.

"This belonged to my father. I thought you might need it. I've rinsed and filled it. If anyone asks, I'll say you took it while I was dozing. There's a small compass attached to the strap, as you can see. I'm sorry that I don't have a suitable map."

I pulled Mwarai's from my pocket. "I actually did steal this."

"So much the better for my story. Please be careful, Owen."

# CHAPTER TWENTY

Ruth's brother's name was Bakaru, and his farm was the most prosperous looking one I'd seen in the valley. Everyone was hard at work when we arrived, including children I recognized as wards of the mission. That made Basil's fondness for my company a little less flattering.

Bakaru, a bow-legged man with fewer surviving teeth than Joseph Wamba sported, congratulated me on my capture of Basil and immediately assigned him to the garden-hoeing detail. Somehow, though, the boy contrived to be within earshot when I interviewed Ruth.

The cook was seated at one of four spinning wheels set up behind the main house. She and the other kerchiefed operators stopped their work as I wound my way through a queue of large baskets filled with raw wool the color of cigar ash. None of the women started up again, which was disappointing. Despite the urgency of my business, I would like to have seen actual spinning being done. Ruth denied me that chance to stall.

"Where is Father Phil?" she demanded. Her bent back made her look awkward at the wheel, like an adult trying to squeeze into a third grader's desk on parents' night. Her broad, plain face was beaded with sweat, but her big eyes were as dry as I'd seen them.

"He's still in jail," I said.

"Why don't you get him out?"

I was so surprised by the anger of this formerly meek

woman that I wondered whether Bakaru provided shots of *changa'a* as part of his employee benefits package. Ruth's assertiveness might simply have been the result of her having a support group handy. The other spinners were murmuring in agreement around me.

"I'm trying to get him out," I said. "That's why I'm here. I think you can help me."

"How?"

It was just as well to start off with a little of the thoroughness Mwarai had attributed to me earlier. "Tell me about anything you saw or heard last night."

"Last night? I saw nothing. Father Phil was cross with me for not seeing you go. For not knowing where you were. Dinner was all spoiled because of you. It was stew. I could have kept it hot. Father Phil said no. He said to feed it to the children. You could eat cold beans when you got back."

That sounded right. "Go on."

"Etta and I ate with the children. I heard Father Phil go off in his jeep. It was dark when I heard the jeep come back."

I stopped her. "You didn't hear anything between the time the jeep left and when it came back?"

"I heard the children."

My experience of Nihuru children was that they were a pretty quiet bunch. That and the first shy look I'd seen on Ruth's face this visit persuaded me to wait her out.

After looking to each of her coworkers in turn, Ruth said, "I heard a laugh. I thought it came from the mission house."

"When was this?"

"Just after sunset."

"What kind of laugh?"

"I don't know. A short one. A loud one. It maybe came from in front of the mission house."

"Man or woman's?"

"A man's laugh. Not Father Phil."

That went without saying. "A big man?"

"I think so."

"Wauki?"

"I don't know. How could I know?"

"You didn't go to see who it was?"

"No. I knew it wasn't Father Phil. It maybe came from the road."

At the rate the laugh was moving away, it would be in Nairobi soon. I gave up that line. "What happened when the jeep came back?"

Ruth seized the new topic with obvious relief. "I went to the house to prepare a meal for Father Phil. As I entered the back of the house, he came through from the front, walking like a drunken man. His face was the color of the moon. He told me to go back to the children and stay with them. He told me something very bad had happened. I went away like he told me. I stayed with the children until Samuel Mwarai arrived."

"Did Father Phil have any blood on his clothes or hands?"

"No," Ruth said emphatically.

That sounded more useful than it really was. Back when he'd been my biggest problem, Mwarai had theorized that Swickard washed himself in the river and changed his clothes after committing the murder. That would be part of any report Gathitu approved. The report could explain away the fact that the jeep hadn't been heard around the time the murder must have occurred by saying that Swickard had parked it out of earshot, only returning for it when he'd washed and dressed and was ready to "discover" the body. Or the report might simply omit the testimony of a cook, if it happened to be inconvenient.

"I went back to wait with the children," Ruth repeated.

"The police came. One of them asked me questions. I told him everything. Now I have told you. There is nothing else to tell."

"Let's talk about Mugo then. How do I find him?"

That brought another chorus of rumbling from the idle spinners and a return of Ruth's earlier belligerence. "Mugo? Mugo cannot help Father Phil."

"Mugo is Father Phil's enemy. Didn't you tell me that? He may have made this trouble for Father Phil."

"Then he will not help you," Ruth said, plainly exasperated with me.

She was actually making a pretty good point. If Mugo was behind the murder, the best I could hope for from him was a curt dismissal. Even if Mugo had nothing to do with Wauki's death and the attacks on the farms, he would probably be disinclined to help the emissary of a Western priest.

But I had no other clue to follow that wouldn't tangle me with Mwarai and Gathitu and land me in jail. For all I knew, they were already looking for me. And I genuinely wanted to meet Mugo, to ask him about the image he'd used to describe me: the hunter who no longer believed in his prey.

I said, "I'll have to trick Mugo into telling me the truth. Maybe with your nephew Daniel's help."

I threw the last part in to stem the doubtful look spreading across Ruth's face. It didn't work. "Go to Nairobi," she said. "Get help for Father Phil there. Go to America."

Get out, in other words, while you still can. "Have you heard from your nephew since he joined Mugo?"

"No." No hesitation or furtive looks with that answer.

"Have you sent him any messages? Any food or clothing?"

"No," Ruth said, her patience slipping another notch. "How could I? He is in the forest, beyond the river."

She pointed to the south. I was still hoping for something

a little more precise. I took out my stolen map.

"Could you show me on this? Is there a road I can follow?"

She wouldn't even look at the map. "Go to Nairobi. Get help there." From her tone, she might have been suggesting psychiatry.

Bakaru came by then to see what was holding up yarn production. Ruth and the others got busy in a hurry, and I reluctantly accepted their foreman's invitation to move along.

Somehow Basil had snuck back to the garden patch he'd been detailed to hoe without getting his ear bent by Bakaru. I stopped there to tell him good-bye. He wasn't having any.

"*I* know where Mugo is," he said, touching his chest with his fist in the Roman salute he liked to use.

"You? How?"

"I followed Daniel to Mugo's camp the night he ran away."

"Why?"

"I heard a noise. I came outside and saw Daniel climbing out of his window. I followed him."

I might have myself at Basil's age, but then I'd had an overdose of the Hardy Boys that Basil had been spared. Still skeptical, I asked, "No one missed you?"

"I was back by dawn."

That was a comforting detail. It made Basil's story a little more credible and placed Mugo's camp this side of Tanzania.

"Tell me how to get there."

The boy suddenly began to hoe furiously. I turned and saw Bakaru approaching on his rounds. He was tapping one bowed leg with a switch as he walked.

"Go that way," Basil whispered, pointing with the hoe. "Wait at the river. I will meet you there."

## CHAPTER TWENTY-ONE

Basil actually beat me to the river. The road I followed from the farm ended at a substantial plank bridge. My guardian and guide stood on the near side of the span, his legs spread slightly and his fists on his hips: the four-foot-tall colossus of Somolet. The strap of a canvas bag hung around his neck and a formidable knife weighed down his tattered shorts. Both were almost certainly Mr. Bakaru's property, so I'd started Basil on a life of crime. At that moment, I was more worried by the realization that he expected to come along.

"You're a regular Houdini," I said in greeting.

"Who?" Basil asked.

I sounded the name out for him. "He was a man who escaped from things. Got out of places when it looked like he couldn't get out."

"Houdini," Basil said, making the name sound distinctly Kenyan. Then he treated me to one of his rare smiles.

"What's in the bag?"

Basil opened the sack, displaying what looked like two pounds of parched corn. "Lunch," he said.

And dinner and breakfast, too, judging by the quantity. I began to doubt my optimistic estimate of the coming hike.

"Thanks," I said, extending my hand for the bag.

"I will carry it," Basil said.

"You're not coming this time. You can show me the way on the map."

"I don't know the way on the map. I only know the way."

"It's too dangerous, Basil."

"I am not afraid. Are you afraid?"

"Yes," I said, surprising and, I knew, disappointing him. "But I have to go. You have to get back."

I saw then that I'd have to take him back to Bakaru's *shamba*, dragging all the way. He anticipated that move, skipping lightly away from me across the bridge.

"I will lead," he called back to me. "Follow if you can."

I didn't have much choice, though it didn't bode well for my plan to con Mugo that I'd been outsmarted by a ten-year-old. We crossed the Nihuru River, muddy and unmighty at that point, with Basil twenty feet ahead of me and so contemptuous of the idea that I'd catch him that he barely bothered to glance over his shoulder. We left the road almost immediately thereafter, heading southwest, according to the late colonel's compass.

The land was brown and dry and rolling, with thickets of thorn bushes in the low spots. The bushes looked dead, but then almost everything did below a certain point in the widely scattered trees. Here and there we glimpsed the reason: grazing animals, but not in the numbers I'd seen from the air. The small groups gave us plenty of traveling room, if they took note of us at all. I saw zebra and, far in the distance, a family of giraffes, moving like a slow-motion mirage. Other little herds I couldn't identify. Basil could, I was sure, but we weren't speaking. I was still officially mad at him, and he was staying so far ahead now that conversation would have been difficult in any case.

He wasn't just staying out of my reach. He was scouting or playing at scouting. It frightened me that I couldn't tell which. He was certainly paying careful attention to each grove of trees we passed on what had become fairly open country. Once he trotted over to examine a stand of trees, signaling for me to wait where I was. When he returned, I extended the canteen and an olive branch with it.

"We lost yet?" I asked.

He shook his head at that but accepted the drink, walking right up to me to do it. We both knew by then that there was no turning back.

After that we walked side by side, still heading southwest. As we walked, we enjoyed a little of the parched corn, which tasted like the sweepings of a very old movie theater.

I asked Basil to tell me what he remembered of Chief Constable Mwarai's interrogation of the wounded men and women in Agat. There was little that hadn't been included in Chief Wamba's English summary. The scattered farms had been completely surprised by the well-armed, well-organized men. Their intent had been to drive the people away, but they hadn't hesitated to fire on anyone who resisted.

In exchange for this report, Basil requested some story-telling. "Have you ever escaped?" was how he phrased it.

Had I ever escaped? From about everyone and everything in my life, I thought. From everything but the questing that had blighted my life, in fact. And I still planned to escape from that, once Swickard was safe. "Yes," I said.

"Tell me of an escape."

"Okay. Back when Father Swickard and I were in school together, I got myself hit on the head and tied up in a barn."

"Who did this?"

"A bad man. A friend of mine was tied up with me. My best friend."

"Yes," Basil said, meaning so far so good. "How did you escape?"

"A little girl helped us. The daughter of the bad man. She was younger than you are. She set fire to another building. Then she cut our ropes."

There was more story to tell—how we'd crawled out through a hole in the barn, how we'd hot-wired my car, how we'd driven out past the burning shed, how the little girl had grown up to be a doctor—but Basil pulled the plug.

"Tell me another story of how you escaped. No little girls."

He'd altered our course very slightly to the south, toward a single tree that had appeared in the distance as we topped a rise.

I considered and discarded the story of my escape from the bottom of an old well. I'd been rescued in that instance by an elderly, emotionally damaged woman. I didn't think Basil would find her any more appealing than the junior pyromaniac.

"I got out of a forest once," I said. That one seemed appropriate somehow.

Basil agreed. "Tell me of that."

"An old man stranded me there."

"A bad man?"

"A man who was a little crazy from living all by himself. A hermit. A storyteller."

"A storyteller," Basil repeated, impressed.

"He led me into his forest to tell me a story. When my back was turned, he slipped away."

The boy emitted a sound that might have been the Nihuru equivalent of a sigh. I decided that it was just as well he knew the worst about my woodcraft, given our destination.

"Where I grew up, there were no forests. No big ones. I wasn't used to being alone in one."

"You were afraid?"

"Yes," I said. Scared to the point of gibbering, as near as I could recall. But then, the week leading up to that forest jaunt had been a hard one for me. Almost as hard as the current week.

"It was getting dark," I said, trying for some expiation. "And the wind was blowing. And I'd heard there was a ghost in that part of the forest."

"A ghost?" Basil asked, and I knew he'd forgiven my timidity.

"The ghost of a pilot who had crashed his plane in those woods many years before."

"How did you escape the ghost?"

I'd walked out. I'd grabbed my rattled nerves by their collective throat, figured out the direction to the nearest road, and walked to it. But that ending wouldn't satisfy my audience. I seized on the fact that Basil had asked how I'd escaped the ghost, not the forest.

"I solved the mystery of why the pilot had crashed. No one else had been able to do that. Not in all the years since it had happened."

Basil knew his basic ghost lore. "And then the pilot was at peace," he pronounced.

I had no idea. I had been at peace for a time. Until the next mystery had come along.

The tree we were making for was a pretty remarkable one. When I'd first taken note of it, I'd estimated that it was perhaps a mile away. We walked that mile, and the tree seemed only slightly nearer. Given our discussion of ghosts, it would have taken very little coaxing to get me thinking that the tree was moving away, like the phantom laugh Ruth claimed to have heard. Beyond the elusive tree lay Mugo's forest. It had been visible almost since we'd left the bridge, but as an unthreatening green band beneath the horizon of mountain peaks. Now we were close enough to see variations in the green, to see the tops of individual trees reaching up above the mass. To see what we were up against when it came to finding Mugo's camp.

I went back to contemplating the single intermediate tree we never seemed to be reaching. The secret of its elusiveness turned out to be its size. Its deceptive size, since it consisted not in amazing height but in really impressive girth. While the tree's canopy was almost wispy, the trunk was massive and misshapen, like poor Chief Wamba's swollen legs. When at length we drew very close, I saw that it was amazing the tree was alive at all. The lower third of its bark appeared to have been eaten away by insects or animals.

Basil's expertise being at my service again, I asked him what the tree was called.

"Baobab," he said. "Very old."

We paused for a drink and a rest in the tree's thin shade. Then Basil took a sighting from the tree to the barely visible peak of what might have been an extinct volcano. We set out toward it, walking due south.

There was nothing to distract me now from the view of the looming forest. I'd come to Kenya looking for a place to disappear, and here it was, a place where few would think to look for me and no one would ever find me. Though I had Basil to look after and Swickard to rescue, the tug of that green belt was so strong my steps quickened and the hot wind on my back felt like an urging hand.

# CHAPTER TWENTY-TWO

Basil might have been feeling his own emotional stirrings, now that the forest was all but towering over us. Or it might simply have been boredom that led him to request another story, tugging on my shirt sleeve to get my attention.

"Another escape?" I asked.

"A murder story," he said.

The renewed impulse I was feeling to step off the face of the earth was a natural link to one murder story, the one that had led to the suicide of a young woman, dark featured and dark souled, in a Boston hotel suite. The sights and smells of Wauki's murder scene had forced me to relive the awful aftermath of that moment. Now Basil's request offered me the chance to revisit the time before the shot, to tell the story of the murder that had brought it all about. But I had no desire to paraphrase that case for Basil's entertainment. Those terrible events had been, in large part, my fault. I'd already lost enough of the boy's respect for one shift.

"How about another ghost story?" I asked.

"Yes, a ghost story."

Luckily I had one ready to hand, one as comforting as those memories of the bloody Boston hotel suite were unnerving. Comforting because the story involved my old friend Harry Ohlman, the lawyer whose suitcase I'd left in Nairobi, and his daughter, Amanda. I would have given a lot to have seen those two just then.

"This happened a few years ago. I was fishing with a

friend and his daughter."

Basil interrupted accusingly. "A little girl?"

"Not that little. Her name is Amanda. You'd like her. She's very brave. Her father is a big man, like Major Praed. An important man. His name is Harry."

"He is a fisherman?"

"No. He's a minor chief. But he likes to fish. Have you ever been fishing?"

"Yes."

"From a boat?"

"No."

"This was a big boat, with a space for meals and a space for sleeping." I found that I was almost as homesick just then for the soft bunks of the *Velvet Noose* as I was for Harry and Amanda. I didn't mention the boat's name to Basil. I didn't feel up to the challenge of explaining the Yuppie sense of humor.

"An ocean boat?" Basil asked.

"Sometimes. That day we were in a bay, as big as all the land you and I have walked. Great Egg Bay."

The boy solemnly repeated the silly, colonial-sounding name, nodding.

"On one side of the bay, on a point of land, was a deserted cannery, a place where they used to put fish into cans."

"I know tuna fish," Basil said with the worldliness I'd come to cherish.

"Everyone around the bay knew that this old cannery was haunted."

Actually, only Amanda and I knew it. We'd invented the haunting as a way to pass the time during fishing trips on the bay. Our storytelling irritated Harry, which was a lot of what had kept the game alive.

"The day was cloudy and the wind and water were very

still." Picturing all that water, brackish though it was, started me thinking of a drink. I made my thirst worse by adding, "It felt like rain was coming."

"Yes," Basil said.

"The boat wasn't anchored. We were drifting as we fished, and the current was taking us down toward the old cannery. It wasn't only old; it was crumbling. Part of it had been burned in a fire. Part had just fallen down. It wasn't a place anybody would be. But as we drifted down on the point, we saw someone."

Amanda had spotted the figure and had warned me with a poke in the ribs that she was up to no good.

"The person who saw it first pointed and said, 'A ghost.'"

"What kind of ghost?"

"An old woman's. She had long, straight hair, like a girl's but white, and her eyes were very hard to see."

"She had no eyes?"

"We couldn't tell at that distance, not even with binoculars. The face seemed almost blank and as white as the long hair. She was standing on the very tip of the point, staring out to sea. Someone had piled up huge rocks there, to keep the sea from wearing the point away. The ghost stood right on the top of one of those rocks."

"What did you do?"

"We decided to investigate."

The fishing had been lousy anyway. Harry had secretly been as bored as his daughter and me. And he'd grown up on the Hardy Boys himself.

"The man who owned the boat, Harry, didn't believe in ghosts. He wanted to prove that the cannery wasn't haunted. He started the boat—"

"But it wouldn't start and you drifted down onto the ghost and the big rocks."

Even a kid from Kenya could improve on my stories' suspense. "No," I said. "The engine started fine. Harry headed for an old concrete landing where the fishing boats used to tie up. As we got closer, I looked for the ghost, to see if I could make out her eyes, but she had disappeared."

"Ah," Basil said.

"Harry was able to get the boat in close because the water was so calm."

Calm, but not dead calm. The *Noose*, all fenders in place, had still been bobbing up and down on the swell when Harry announced that we would have to jump the remaining gap.

"We couldn't tie up to the landing without hurting the boat, so Harry and I jumped across the water." Neither of us had made a pretty job of it—Harry because he had a bad leg—but we'd stayed dry.

"Who was steering the boat?"

"The young woman, Amanda," I said, aging her slightly to soften the blow. "She grew up on boats. She knows boats the way you know this valley." The way I hope you know this valley, I added to myself.

"Amanda drove the boat a little way off and waited for us."

"Then what did you do?"

"We split up."

"*Split up*?"

I wasn't sure whether Basil was unfamiliar with the idiom or expressing his disapproval of the plan. I'd often voiced a similar objection while watching a movie or a television show in which two characters separated in the face of a hidden danger, a monster or an ax murderer. I'd had those very misgivings that day on the landing, but I seldom gave the orders in Harry's presence.

"Yes, we separated. Harry went out to search the rocks on the point. I went to look inside the cannery."

This time Basil didn't ask me if I'd been afraid. He was taking it for granted by then.

"There was only one place I could search, only one building still standing. All the windows had been broken out and the door knocked down, so I was able to walk right in."

I didn't mention the graffiti spray painted on the old brick walls or the little pockets of garbage that had collected in every corner the wind couldn't scour clean. Or the smell of the place. It had probably been a combination of rotting seaweed and bird dung, but it had suggested that a giant pile of fish heads from the cannery's glory days was somewhere upwind.

In fact, I didn't mention anything else about the haunted cannery. Not then. We'd reached the shadow of the forest, and I could see that Basil had lost his bearings.

His mountain peak goal had been out of sight for some time, blocked by the tree tops, but he'd kept us on a straight course using a detail of the forest itself: a tree that had been struck by lightning. We'd been able to walk to the very base of this tree, the beginning of the forest being quite abrupt, with almost no warning fringe of saplings or brush. I decided that the grazing animals were what kept it edged like a suburban flower bed.

There was obviously no way to breach the green wall at the point where we stood. Not without machetes. Basil turned to his left, to the east, and we began to trace the edge of the forest. I consulted my watch. We'd left the Nihuru River behind us over three hours earlier. If we wanted to get back in daylight, we'd have to start soon. Give up and head back to house arrest or worse.

I asked, "How far to Mugo's camp?"

Basil gave his stock answer. "Not far."

"You say you got all the way out here and back in only

one night?"

"Yes."

"It's a long way to walk in one night."

"I did not walk back," Basil said. "I ran."

I started to ask what had caused him to run and decided the question could wait.

We walked east for about ten minutes. Then Basil turned us around and headed us back toward the shattered tree. From there, we walked west. The forest bulged outward slightly causing us to detour a little to the north. Beyond the bulge, the ground sloped away, and Basil quickened our pace. Soon we came to what he'd evidently been searching for all along: a tiny stream. It flowed from the forest and beside it ran a narrow path.

Basil entered the forest without a backward glance. I followed, glancing backward every few feet. My guide indicated that we were not to speak, but conversation would have been difficult now in any case. The path was too narrow for us to walk side by side. And the wind in the trees created a sound like a not-too-distant waterfall. Despite that background noise and the steady calling of birds—visible only as flashes of color: green and gold and even blue—I could hear the clomp of my boots on the packed earth of the path. I was sure that Mugo could hear it if he wasn't actually feeling it.

Earlier in our walk I'd described getting lost in the New Jersey Pine Barrens, so it was inevitable that I'd start comparing this forest to that one of memory. They didn't have much in common, beyond the ferns that carpeted both, though these Kenyan ferns, huge and lush, would have been running things in the Barrens in no time. I remembered the Jersey trees as ruining each other's shapes in their competition for the light. Here that competition didn't really start until high above our heads, a hundred feet and more. The trunks beneath the tangled ceiling were thin and straight and graceful, a few so pale they were almost white. Contrasting with this grace and order were the vines that grew up unlucky trees, some heavy with thorns, some flowering madly.

Basil paused only once, to yield the right-of-way to a mottled snake that made a noise like a startled steam engine when we happened upon it. The boy never looked back, but then he had my steady clomping to reassure him. I continued to look back frequently. On one of those backward glances, I saw a man following us on the path.

Though I did a double take that wrenched my neck, there was nothing particularly threatening about the man. He was tall and thin and, like Basil, dressed only in shorts. I could see he carried no weapon. He wasn't overtaking us but pacing us, staying a steady twenty yards back.

Rattled as I was, I hadn't stopped walking. Now I collided with Basil, who had stopped. Twenty yards ahead of us on the path was the twin of the man behind us.

I looked back and saw that our shadow had stopped when we stopped. We all four stood for a moment, sizing one another up. Then the man in front resumed walking in the direction we'd been heading. The rest of us played follow the leader, maintaining our previous generous spacing.

After five minutes, our procession entered a little clearing. A white tent was pitched on the clearing's far side. In the center of the space was a round fire pit. Next to the pit stood a very small man whose white robes shone, even against the background of the tent. Mugo the mystic.

"Owen Keane, I presume," he said and tittered at his joke.

## CHAPTER TWENTY-THREE

Major Praed had said that almost any man wearing the narrow-chested Swickard's shirt would have to have left it unbuttoned. Mugo was an exception. He could have worn the priest's shirt as a bathrobe. I'd heard him compared to Gandhi, and the similarities were inescapable and perhaps intentional. Though he wore no spectacles, Mugo did affect a shaven head. Of course, the white attire was another link, in color at least. In style there were variations on the Gandhi pattern. Around his tiny body, Mugo wore what looked like a white sarong. Over his shoulders was draped another white cloth, like an oversize shawl. The air in the forest was cooler than that of the arid grassland we'd just crossed. It appeared to be very cool to the mystic, who stayed close to the small fire. He also stood in a patch of sunlight, either for additional warmth or because it made his white outfit glow. Chesney had mentioned his weakness for theatrics.

Like Joseph Wamba, Mugo might have arranged for the murder of Wauki but he couldn't have wielded the sword himself. In the mystic's case, it was because he couldn't have lifted it. I'd seen at least two of his followers who could have done the killing: our escorts along the forest path. Both men had melted back into the trees as soon as Basil and I reached the clearing, leaving us alone with their leader, who beckoned us closer to the fire pit.

"I've been expecting you, you see," Mugo said. "I am very pleased that you made the journey safely. Though, with this one leading you," he smiled toward Basil, "you could make it to Mombasa itself." He spoke English with a very BBC accent, supporting Chesney's deduction that he'd been educated in England. "Tea will be ready presently. Please sit down. I have no chair to offer you, but perhaps the soft earth of the forest won't be too unattractive after your epic trek."

It wasn't. Basil and I sat on one side of the fire and Mugo on the other, the mystic settling cross-legged in his sun spotlight and arranging the ends of his shoulder cloth so they covered his knees. That left only his head, upper chest and hands exposed. Using them, I tried to guess his age and failed. His very dark skin was unwrinkled and unlined, but his small melancholy eyes were anything but youthful.

I found my voice at last. "How did you know we were coming?"

"Once you neared the forest, you were seen, of course. But I've heard much of you since your arrival, Mr. Keane. I have my many sources. I was even able to observe you once in person, though the opportunity for an introduction did not present itself. I knew a man of your curiosity, of your spiritual bent shall we say, would make the pilgrimage with your two companions sooner or later."

"My two companions?"

"Yes. This boy with the heart of a lion. And the one who came with you from America. The spirit of the sad dark girl that has accompanied you everywhere. The Nihuru are quite familiar with the spirits of the dead. They call such a spirit a *ngoma*. Your *ngoma* has been widely reported to me."

"Do you expect me to believe that?"

"An interesting question, Mr. Keane. From what I'm told, you're a man without beliefs, so the obvious answer is no. But I've always felt, in common with that Englishman Chesterton, that a man who refuses to believe in the divine is very likely to believe in anything else. I would never try to convince a devout Christian that the spirit of a dead girl was sitting beside him, had her hand on his shoulder, in fact. Ah, I see you shiver. Please forgive my terrible lapse in manners. Here is our tea."

A young man had emerged from the trees behind the tent. Improbably, he carried a gleaming white teapot and a small wicker case. He placed the pot in the ashes of the fire. Then he opened the case, revealing cups and saucers and silver-ware, all secured with leather straps.

"Tea is one of my few indulgences," Mugo said to ac-company the unpacking. "I hope it is also one of yours."

In an effort to steady myself, I studied the young man doing the unpacking. Unlike Mugo's other minions, this one owned a shirt, a white one that needed washing. And he'd been shaving without the benefit of a mirror recently. What confirmed my hunch was the effort Basil was devoting to rudely ignoring the newcomer.

"Hello, Daniel," I said. "I'll tell your aunt you're look-ing well."

"Thank you," Daniel said.

"You're welcome to come back with us, if you'd like. I know Father Swickard would be happy to see you."

"Thank you," the young man said again, but this time it was just a formality. He was pouring the tea by then, starting with mine and then Basil's.

When his turn came, Mugo said, "I'm sorry we don't have any of those bread and butter sandwiches that Miss Chesney likes to serve," demonstrating that his sources of informa-tion were indeed very good, if I needed any further proof.

I was considering his sources at that moment, as it hap-pened, trying to figure out how he'd heard of that death in Boston and the effect it had had on me. I'd only discussed it with one person since coming to Kenya, the man who currently resided in the Somolet jail. But Swickard might have told others, perhaps even Mugo himself. Or we might have been overheard discussing the suicide that first afternoon on the mission porch, by a spy sent for that purpose or by Etta or even by Ruth, the woman who had been so against my visiting Mugo, the woman whose nephew now hovered over us like the perfect butler.

Just coming up with some possible explanations for Mugo's knowledge of the dead girl calmed me remarkably. I was ready to take the offensive when the mystic inquired after Swickard.

"I was so sorry to hear of the good father's arrest. His faith is sustaining him, I am sure."

"I'm sure you couldn't care less," I said bluntly. "You're no friend of Father Swickard's. You lured his assistant away from him. That ruined Father Swickard's dream of passing on his mission to a Nihuru priest. And it isolated him at a very dangerous time."

Mugo sipped his tea. "Luckily you came to relieve that isolation, Mr. Keane. Interesting that your arrival didn't keep what was fated to happen from happening. I'm something of a fatalist, I'm afraid. So you see me as Father Swickard's enemy?"

"Why did you come to Somolet last night?"

"A number of us were drawn there last night," Mugo replied. "There are places where, at certain moments in time, unseen streams converge, drawing men together like the water of this valley is drawn to the Nihuru. You and Chief Constable Mwarai were drawn to the same place last night, for example. As were Major Praed and Dr. Brocious."

"You said you'd had an opportunity to observe me. You were watching the mission when Major Praed brought me in."

Mugo nodded. "With all the lights and confusion, I was able to go quite unnoticed."

"You didn't happen to be on hand when your unseen streams drew Wauki and his murderer together, did you?"

"Regrettably no. Nor was I in time to witness Father Swickard's discovery of the body. If I had, I assure you I would have come forward to second his story. Despite what you've been told, I bear the priest no ill will."

He tsked a very delicate tsk. "I see that you do not believe me. Perhaps we should begin with the matter of Daniel. You say I lured him away from the mission. The truth is, he came to me of his own free will, almost six months ago. Is that not true, Daniel?"

"It is true."

"Six months ago?" I asked. "Why?"

I asked Daniel, but Mugo answered. "Why does any man seek out a teacher? To learn what he has to teach. I accepted Daniel as my student, but sent him back to the mission."

"To spy?"

"No, Mr. Keane. To learn all that the priest had to teach. And not so Daniel could use that knowledge against Christians in some future struggle, to anticipate your next charge. The struggle I foresee, the struggle for which I wish Daniel to be prepared, is not between men of faith."

"Who is it between?"

"There are only two sides as far as I am concerned. Belief and non-belief. Father Swickard believes in the divine. I believe in the divine. Therefore we are on the same side. All men of faith are on the same side. All the practitioners of the great religions and the practitioners of the very humble, very ancient ones, like myself.

"Do not mistake me. There are certainly doctrinal differences that divide us. Differences as numerous as the trees of this forest. Differences that men of bad faith or no faith exploit to keep believers distrustful of one another."

That sounded familiar. "Like the tribes of Kenya?"

"Precisely. Divide and conquer, an old tactic. It keeps the Kenyan tribes from coming together to form a truly great nation. It keeps men of faith from coming together to find the common threads of their traditions and following those threads to a single truth. That is what I do in the quiet of this forest. I reflect on a lifetime's study of the history of human faith, looking for those common threads."

"Chief Wamba thinks you're worshipping trees."

"I'm sure that forward-thinking man considers me little better than a witch doctor. Quite understandably. I have encouraged certain stories to be told about me, both to explain my presence and to ensure that my solitude would be undisturbed."

"Like your contempt for all things modern and Western?"

The mystic bowed. "That part of my reputation is a natural result of my lifestyle. But as you can see," he raised his teacup, "I am not unpolluted."

Daniel refilled my own cup then, not for the first time. The tea wasn't exactly perking me up. The warm liquid or the smoke of the fire or the drone of the forest was making me very sleepy. I fought it off.

"Father Swickard believes you're reintroducing the old spiritual beliefs."

"Actually, I'm researching them. Questioning people about their ancestors' practices might revive interest in those practices, but that is only a side effect. I am a theorist, not an advocate."

"If you're just a theorist, why do you need a network of spies? And what were you doing out by Agat yesterday?"

"The issue of the land theft interests me. At first it was

only because it so aptly mirrored my conception of the world of faith, where brother is encouraged to fight brother over trifles. But lately, inspired in part by the example of your friend Father Swickard, I have begun to feel that I must leave my monkish cell and become more engaged, to learn more of this threat to my people."

"Your people? You're not a Nihuru."

"I never claimed to be. That would be to think as the opposition would have us think. Of factions. Of differences. All people are my people. That is what my meditations have led me to believe.

"But I see you are fatigued. You must rest before dinner. I eat rather late, as a rule. You will be my guests, of course."

"We have to get back," I said, with a thick tongue. "The police—"

Mugo raised a tiny hand. "I must insist. The journey is far too dangerous at night. And we have only just begun our talk. Besides which, your guide is unavailable."

He gestured toward Basil, who had curled up on the mossy ground and gone to sleep. His teacup was resting upside down beside him.

I looked at my own cup in panic. Mugo tittered again. "You haven't been drugged, Mr. Keane. Nor has your friend. Young lion!"

Basil sat up, blinking.

"You see? It is merely physical exhaustion combined with nervous strain. Rest now," he said, fixing me with a stare like a movie vampire's. "I must meditate before we eat."

## CHAPTER TWENTY-FOUR

With Daniel's help, I carried the dozing Basil to the tent and settled him onto one of its two canvas cots. The runaway assistant didn't hold the boy's earlier rudeness against him, handling him gently like the old friend he was. He would have tucked him in, I was sure, if there had been anything to tuck. But the cots had no bedding.

Daniel showed no signs of his aunt's bent back. Or her open, disingenuous eyes. The lower portion of his narrow head was shaved, but no more evenly than his chin. On top his hair rose up in uneven clumps, giving him the look of a man awakened suddenly from a dream. He acted that way, too, shifting his weight from foot to foot and peering around.

I sat down on the second cot, which was a mistake. The taut canvas felt softer than any bed I could remember, and I didn't have time to spare for a nap.

"Is that how it happened?" I asked the young man. "You came to Mugo and he sent you back to the mission?"

"Yes," he said, "to learn."

To question Swickard and to observe him so closely that the lonely priest mistook the zeal for a budding vocation. In a way, he'd been right.

"Why did you leave?"

"The master recalled me. He said it was time."

"Time for what?"

"Simply time," Daniel said. "Now you should rest."

He didn't have Mugo's snake-charming act down. I found

it was easier to resist his powers of suggestion. "Sorry to be moving you out of the tent," I said.

"I do not sleep here," Daniel replied a little wistfully.

With that prompting, I noticed that the ground around the cots wasn't particularly worn. "This was set up for our visit?"

"As he said, the master knew you would come."

A man of my curiosity and spiritual bent. Or curiously bent spirituality. Once, when I was closer to Daniel's age, I might have run away to join Mugo myself. In a sense, I had run away in search of a master, a gatherer of threads, a mystic with a single answer. Now I found I didn't have much interest in Mugo's quest for a unifying theory. I wondered if that was a sign that I'd finally escaped the one thing I'd never been able to escape. If so, it put getting out of a barn or a well or a forest in the minor leagues.

As Daniel withdrew, I lay back on the cot to think about it and promptly fell asleep. When I awoke, the tent was dark except for a flickering light just visible through its almost closed flaps. I nudged Basil.

"Round two," I said.

I was actually expecting dinner to be some kind of major production, but Mugo the performance artist was nothing if not a minimalist. The fire had been built up to several times the size of that afternoon's smoky tea warmer. Otherwise, the clearing was unchanged. Mugo hadn't even shifted his position in relationship to the fire pit. In fact, he appeared not to have moved through all the time we'd slept, but that might just have been the impression he was trying to create.

As Basil and I resumed our earlier places, I sensed that one thing about the mystic had changed. It was his mood. Mugo seemed distracted, and his earlier cheerfulness was gone. I asked what was bothering him.

"Perhaps nothing," he said. "Forgive my wandering

mind. You must also forgive what I'm afraid will be a very simple repast."

He raised a hand, and Daniel appeared out of the darkness, carrying a small pot. It seemed that dinner, like the earlier tea, had been prepared elsewhere. In all likelihood, we hadn't been taken to Mugo's camp after all, but to a neutral site set up especially for our meeting. Evidently the mystic trusted me about as much as I trusted him.

He was still on the subject of the menu. "It is only humble *ugali*, a dish made of maize. I am sorry that we are not able to offer you the bread you enjoyed yesterday evening at the Ngatini *shamba*," he added, showing off his knowledge of my movements again, this time without much zest. "Our *ugali* is flavored with roots and certain other gifts of my forest. Make a paste of it with your fingers, as the boy is doing. I think you will find it piquant."

After our forced march on water and parched corn, I would have found cold oatmeal piquant. Basil and I were digging into our wooden bowls with a will when Mugo spoke again. "You have had time to reflect, Mr. Keane. Do you find that you believe what I told you this afternoon?"

"I believe what you told me about Daniel," I said.

"That is a start."

"Why did you recall him?"

"An inkling, an intimation of danger. Though the image is a sinister one to Western minds, I am very like a spider sitting at the center of his web. I sense small movements or vibrations and I interpret them. The vibrations I sensed in this case told me that Daniel would be safer with me."

"Why didn't you warn Father Swickard when you went to the mission to talk with him?"

The only answer I got to that was a small smile, a not particularly pleasing one in the dancing light of the fire.

"What did your vibrations tell you about Wauki?"

"Very little, which to me is quite suggestive."

"Of what, reincarnation?"

"Careful, Mr. Keane. No Christian, not even a fallen-away one, should disparage the idea of a man returning from the grave. The Hindus believe that each of us must experience many lives, many reincarnations before we achieve nirvana, and not all of them human lives. I don't know what they would say of a case like Wauki's, in which a soul returns over and over again as the exact same kind of human. Or rather, as a series of humans who commit the exact same mistake."

"What mistake?"

"A misjudgment of their fellow human beings. But you've no real interest at the moment in Hindu beliefs. I must own to being a little disappointed on that point. Given your reputation, I was looking forward to a lively discussion on a broad spectrum of spiritual topics. Yet all your questions are very worldly."

I'd considered my indifference to Mugo's teachings prior to my nap, seeing it as a sign of my growing up at last, of my finally shedding what Swickard had called my congenital immaturity. But I'd been sleepy then. I was wide awake now, and I wondered if I might be disinterested because I'd recognized, on some subconscious level, that Mugo the comparative religion teacher was too good to be true, too tailor-made for someone with my preoccupations. That this was all an act, in other words, and the explanation he'd given for his presence in the forest a lie.

It would have been bad manners to accuse him of deceiving me while I was eating his maize. So I said, "My friend is in jail."

"Of course that would explain your sad lack of interest in the spiritual. At least since Father Swickard's arrest. But what if we find examples of it from before that arrest? You spoke with Wauki, I believe."

"You know I did."

"Did you ask him about his reincarnation? About his experience of the afterlife?"

"No," I admitted.

"No," Mugo repeated. "You simply weren't interested in such things, even before your friend's misfortune. Forgive me for observing it, but I sense that you may have. . . What is the very apt English expression? Ah, yes. I sense that you may have lost heart. Perhaps because of the *ngoma*, the dark companion we discussed earlier."

He glanced toward the empty air to my right. I resisted a very strong urge to follow his gaze.

Instead, I asked, "What made you go to Agat yesterday? Had you heard the land raiders were going to strike?"

Mugo became distracted again. He watched Daniel spoon out Basil's third helping. Then he said, "Earlier I spoke of my inklings and intimations. I had such an intimation that the attacks might occur. But my timing was poor. I was not on hand to witness those atrocities, to see the faces of the men who committed them. I could have understood it so much better if I could have seen their faces. But it was not to be. As we've already discussed, my arrival at the mission was equally mistimed."

"You had advanced warning of the murder?"

"Not a warning. Nothing so precise. I experienced an uneasiness. A sense of impending spiritual upheaval."

That reminded me of something Chesney had told me. "Like the feeling of spiritual dissonance that brought you to this valley?"

I saw that I'd surprised him for once. "I'd forgotten that I'd mentioned that during my chat with Father Swickard."

I played along. "Are these attacks the cause of that spiritual disturbance? Were you drawn here because of them?"

"It is impossible to say. It is the nature of the unseen streams I mentioned earlier, the streams that carry each man to his destiny, to be inexplicable. Perhaps I was drawn here to become Daniel's teacher. Or perhaps it was to meet you, Owen Keane, a man whose coming I never could have foretold."

"But you did foretell it."

"I beg your pardon."

"You mentioned me to Father Swickard. He said you did, not by name but figuratively. 'The hunter who does not believe in his prey.'"

Mugo looked grave. "Father Swickard interpreted that as a reference to you?" He closed his eyes for a moment. "Yes, I see it. The divine is your prey, the prey you still pursue though years have passed since you believed in it."

He shook his head. "Again you must forgive me, Mr. Keane, you really must. I never imagined there would be two people in Father Swickard's acquaintance suffering from that very dangerous malady."

I started to ask about the other sufferer. Then Basil jumped to his feet and turned to face the tent. A second later, a man rushed out of the forest. He crossed to Mugo, bowed, and began to speak, not in English. I recognized him as one of the matched pair who had intercepted us on the trail. His lean body glistened with sweat in the firelight.

"Momentous news," Mugo said when the man had finished his report. "Word has come of the land raiders. There is to be another attack this very night."

## CHAPTER TWENTY-FIVE

"An attack where?"

"In a distant corner of the valley, but one far more accessible from my forest than the location of the last outrage. I must go and see for myself. You are welcome to spend the night here under Daniel's excellent care. If you choose to leave in the morning, the way will be open to you."

"Basil will stay," I said. "I'll go with you."

"I will go too!" Basil shouted. I knew without looking that he was banging his chest.

"I must agree with the young lion, Mr. Keane. It would not do to separate you two. I would be pleased to have you both at my side. We must leave right away and we must hurry. My information is vague as to which farms will be attacked. Until we are sure, we must follow a middle course."

We set out, Mugo's scout leading, then the mystic, then Basil. I brought up the rear, or the spirit of the dark girl did, unless she'd stayed behind with Daniel.

We carried only what Basil and I had brought with us: the canteen and the bag of corn. Our only weapon was the knife the boy wore on his rope belt. Ahead of us somewhere in the darkness were men with automatic weapons, men Chesney had said would be more than a match for a unit armed with rifles.

Her father's compass had a luminous dial, luckily, the moon being cut off from us by the forest canopy. The trail we were following led west more often than not. I tried to visualize the map of the valley. We were moving roughly parallel to the Nihuru River, but far to the south of it. Moving toward the tip of the leaf-shaped valley, toward the point of the arrowhead.

And at a very rapid pace. I'd assumed it would be no challenge to keep up with the frail mystic, and I'd been wrong. In no time I'd worked out the stiffness left from the afternoon's hike, moved through a brief period of comparative comfort, and then awakened a whole new set of aches. Ominously, the new ones were in my joints, not my muscles. And in my feet. My new boots, which had been fine for hiking, turned out to be poor for speed walking. I should have stopped to tighten their laces, but I had an irrational fear of being left behind by the three Kenyans. Irrational for a man who'd hoped to lose himself in this same forest. Even turns in the trail that briefly hid Mugo's ghostly white form gave me little jolts of panic.

We went on that way for almost two hours. Then Mugo called a brief halt, so brief that we hardly had time to pass the canteen around before we were off again. When we stopped for the second time, a little past midnight, I thought it was just another break. But this time Mugo and his man conferred in very low voices. Then the mystic turned to me.

"The trail branches here, Mr. Keane. We dare not go farther without some definite word. It should have been here waiting for us. Now we must wait for it. Let us make ourselves as comfortable as we can."

I was too tired by then to ask any questions about hunters or prey or spiritual dissonance. Too tired to do anything but slump down next to Basil on the floor of the forest crossroads. The next thing I knew, Mugo was shaking me.

"We have our information, Mr. Keane. Unfortunately, we still have some distance to travel. We may not be in time."

I started to rise, but he held me in place with a hand the size of Basil's. "Wait a moment. Before we set out there is something I must tell you. Something to recompense you for your visit to my forest. I tell you now in case we become separated."

"Tell me what?"

"A name for you to ask about when you return to Somolet. Charles Njagi." He spelled the last name for me. "Can you remember it?"

I repeated it, correct spelling and all.

"Very good."

Our number was now five, not counting *ngomas*. The newcomer, the one who had brought us definite word of the raiders' target, was the second man who had snuck up on Basil and me that afternoon. He took up his familiar station behind me as we plunged on through the black forest. This time, though, he didn't hang back a respectful twenty yards. I could feel him on my heels, silently urging me to keep up.

From the little Mugo had told me, I expected the journey before us to be as long as the trip to the crossroads. But we began to hear gunfire only half an hour later, and it wasn't far off. We broke into a run without a word being spoken. The firing continued in single shots and short bursts.

I could see patches of starry sky through the tree tops, and I realized that the forest was thinning. I'd no sooner had that thought than we arrived at the very edge of the trees, and Mugo was holding us back with outstretched arms. His white shawl was backlit, and not from any staging he'd arranged. A hundred yards beyond the edge of the forest a house was on fire.

The echo of the now stray shots seemed to be coming from well beyond the burning house. From the same direction and distance came men's laughter. Then I heard something that made the first two sounds even more horrible. A woman screaming.

At once I forgot the need to protect Basil and save Swickard. I forgot my irrational fear of being lost in the forest. I didn't feel any fear. Only a longing.

I slipped the canteen from my shoulder and handed it to Basil. "Stay here," I said.

Someone, Mugo or one of the twins, grabbed at my shirt as I broke through the tree line. Grabbed at but didn't stop me.

I crossed the stretch of open ground at a run, coming down hard in unseen depressions and stumbling up little rises. By the time I reached a patch of maize—stunted and dry—I could feel heat from the burning house. Beyond the maize was a tangle of poles and lines, like clotheslines but supporting some kind of vining plants, the broad leaves of which were curling in the heat.

The house was too far gone to enter. I circled it to the right. The screaming that had drawn me there had stopped. I could hear frightened cattle now in addition to the stray shots and laughter. The raiders were shooting the livestock.

I could see the muzzle flashes of their guns, just beyond the light cast by the by fire. I had only to follow those flashes and my journey would be over. I took a single step that way and stumbled against an overturned bench.

A woman was on the other side of it, protected a little from the heat, not that she cared. She'd been shot several times, and her eyes and mouth were open in an expression of everlasting surprise. She lay on her side with her arms stretched out like a diver's. Just beyond her fingers was a bundle in a blanket. As I reached out to touch it, it moved.

From behind me, someone grabbed my sleeve. It was Basil, carrying the hat I'd lost sometime during my stumbling run. His eyes were wide with fear as he tried to pull me back the way we'd come.

I looked one last time at the flashes of light. Then I scooped up the baby. As soon as I did, it began to cry. Basil led the way back around the house. We sprinted into the arbor of vining plants and found our way blocked by a man dressed in army fatigues, smoking a cigarette.

I saw him a second before he saw us, saw that he carried no rifle but wore a holstered pistol, saw a broad scar across his nose, saw his almost bored expression, the expression of a man looking over a potential property for his still distant retirement.

Then he spotted us, and his face went blank. The last thing I saw was his hand reaching for his holster. Basil dodged to the right, and we were in the stunted field of maize, running hard and waiting for pistol shots that never came.

# CHAPTER TWENTY-SIX

"Finish the story of the ghost woman," Basil said. "The woman on the rocks."

It was almost noon of the day following the attack and our escape. Basil, the baby, and I were somewhere in the arid prairie south of the Nihuru River. Exactly where, I had no idea. I'd lost my stolen map, either on my run to the burning farmhouse or earlier, during our line dance through the forest. Not that I could have found us on that map. Or one of Kenya or Africa or the Eastern Hemisphere.

Basil, my personal Global Positioning System, was temporarily off-line. It hadn't happened right away. After we'd run through the maize field and back to the forest, he'd guided me straight to the spot where we'd left Mugo and his escorts. But the three had gone. They'd left behind only the canteen and the bag of corn as proof that the boy hadn't erred.

Basil's troubles had started after that. When I'd asked him if he could find his way back along the forest trails, he'd very emphatically said no. So I'd led us east along the edge of the forest. We'd gotten away before the man in the fatigues could organize a search.

At first we'd stayed close to the trees in case we needed cover in a hurry. I'd decided that we'd stick to our easterly course for several hours, until we were sure of being clear of the raiders. Then we'd head northeast for the Nihuru. At the first *shamba* we passed, we'd find someone to care for the baby.

Only we never passed a *shamba*. It hadn't been light very long before I realized my mistake. I'd taken us too far east before I'd turned us north. We were somewhere in the game lands we'd crossed the afternoon before, when I'd entertained Basil with stories of my adventures.

Now he wanted more. He was bored again, since there was no immediate danger. Bored and jealous of the baby.

The baby was a girl, which had been easy to establish. I was less certain about her age, but I was guessing three months. She wasn't very large, weighing no more than fifteen pounds, but fifteen pounds was the weight of a decent-sized bowling ball, as my shoulders and arms had been reminding me for the last hour. She didn't have any teeth, luckily, or she'd have bitten me early on. Her eyes used up most of her angry face, and, when she didn't have them screwed shut for screaming, they met my own eyes defiantly.

She was naked except for the rough blanket I'd found her in, which was getting smaller. As she soiled parts of it, I was cutting them away with Basil's knife. He would then bury the pieces, either so we couldn't be tracked by them or as an editorial comment.

I'd also cut away part of my shirt tail and tied it in a knot. I was alternately soaking it in the canteen and giving it to the baby to suck on. That provided her with a little water and Basil and me with a rest from her crying.

It was during one of these lulls that the boy requested part two of the mystery of the haunted cannery. I was very tired, and my mouth was dry, but I didn't want to turn him down. He'd been uncharacteristically withdrawn since our escape, not trying to lead and sometimes even holding onto my belt as we walked.

"Where were we?" I asked.

"You jumped off the boat. You and Chief Harry."

"Right." It was a pleasure to think of that cool, overcast day. A pleasure and an exquisite torture.

"You split up," Basil added, still priming the pump. "You went inside the building. What did you find?"

"The ghost."

Actually, I'd first found the remains of the roof, which had tumbled in during some past storm, leaving four brick walls with gaping empty windows. I'd been picking my way around the debris and daydreaming when I'd happened upon her.

"She was hiding in there, sitting on an old block of stone with her hands on her knees, being very quiet."

"And she had no eyes?" Basil asked, reminding me of the juicy conclusion to which I'd allowed him to jump.

"She had eyes. Blue eyes. But they were very pale, paler than the sky is now." The very hot, cloudless sky. I scanned it for the hundredth time, looking for Noah and his old Cessna, my personal T.C. coming to the rescue.

When I looked down, I saw two beautiful brown eyes considering me. The baby's. For the first time, those eyes seemed neither angry or afraid.

Basil was tugging on my sleeve. "The ghost had pale eyes?"

"Yes. That's why we couldn't see her eyes from the boat."

Basil didn't care for that. He'd like it even less, I knew, if I told him she hadn't been a ghost after all, just a frightened old woman. So I didn't tell him. I didn't want him rejecting the story. I was too tired to come up with a replacement.

"What did you do?"

"I asked her what she wanted, why she'd been standing out on the point." I'd coaxed it out of her, after I'd calmed us both. It had helped that she'd mistaken me for somebody who had a right to be there.

"Her name was Dorothy. She told me that she'd worked in the cannery when she was a young woman. She'd fallen in love with a man who worked there. His name was Herman."

That was editing it down and then some. I didn't think Basil would put up with much of Dorothy's tearful reminiscences, not even this new, gentler, more vulnerable Basil.

"Before they could marry, Herman was called away to fight in a war. He was taken across the ocean the cannery faced." Taken to Africa, in fact, though I hadn't remembered that connection when I'd selected the story. "He died in battle."

Yesterday Basil would have asked for the gory details. Today he said, "And Dorothy?"

"She moved far away. She married someone else. Raised a family. Grew old. But she never forgot Herman. And finally, she came back to the cannery."

"After she died," Basil supplied.

After her husband, a pipe fitter, had died. "She came back to where she'd been happiest. She ended up out on the point, staring out to sea, just like she had during the war."

"What did you do?"

"I left her alone."

I'd told her to stay as long as she liked and hurried out to head off Harry. He'd finished searching the point and gone inland to examine the fence that protected the property. I'd caught him on his return trip.

"I didn't want Harry to bother the ghost with his disbelief, so I didn't tell him about her. We went back to the landing. Harry signaled Amanda, and she brought the boat back in."

Like a pro. The tide had been going out the whole time we'd been on the point. Harry and I had fallen more than jumped back into the *Noose*, sending Amanda into hysterics. Still, she'd gotten us away without scratching the paint.

"Harry decided that it was too late to start fishing again. So we headed home. On the way, we cruised out by the point. And there she was."

"The ghost?"

"The ghost, looking out across the ocean again."

"What did Harry say then?"

"He said he believed now that it was a ghost."

Harry had cited his examination of the fence, declaring that no living person could have reached the cannery, except as we had, by boat. I could still feel the little shudder Harry's pronouncement had sent through me in the second before I realized that he was pulling my leg. Mugo was right. I would believe anything. For a while.

"The last time I looked back to the point, she was still there."

"She will always be there," Basil declared. "You didn't give her what she wanted." That must have sounded too critical to him, because he added, "No one could."

"No one could," I said.

The baby had sucked her khaki pacifier dry. I gave it to Basil to soak and offered her a knuckle as a substitute. To my surprise, she accepted it after some token crying. I didn't know whether to be flattered that we were getting on so well or worried that she was too weak to fuss.

I was turning my head so the shade from my hat brim would better cover her face when I saw the dust cloud in the shimmering distance. Beneath it was some kind of vehicle.

"Basil—"

"I know," he said, handing me back the sopping knot of cloth. "It is a jeep."

"You know?"

"I have been watching it. It is coming this way."

"Why didn't you say something?"

"You were telling the story."

There was nowhere to hide, even if we'd been in any condition to pass up a lift. Since we weren't and since the jeep was coming from the east, from the direction of Somolet, I waved my hat over my head.

By then I could hear the engine. The driver appeared to be going flat out, or as near to it as the uneven ground would permit. I was willing the driver to be Dr. Brocious or Major Praed or, better still, Lori Praed, wearing her yellow bikini and carrying a frosty pitcher of orange juice. It was Chief Constable Mwarai.

He and his jeep were both covered with red dust. I decided that they were both overheated, too, guessing about the jeep. Mwarai was out of his seat almost before the vehicle had slid to a stop. He threw his uniform cap on the ground and came at me, hands at the ready. He would have knocked me down next, but the baby saved me. Frightened by the noise and dust of Mwarai's arrival, she started to cry like she had back at the farmhouse.

The sight of her stopped the policeman cold. "What in the name of—"

"A survivor," I cut in, so heartened by her bawling that I was grinning. "The raiders struck again last night."

"How did you— How could you— How—"

"Buy me a cold beer, and I'll tell you all about it."

The policeman dropped his hands to his sides in resignation. I noticed then that he'd been holding his handcuffs. He returned them to his belt.

"Get into the jeep," he ordered.

## CHAPTER TWENTY-SEVEN

Mwarai wouldn't wait for his answers. He drove back at a reasonable speed, treating the baby as I had done at first, like an unexploded bomb. So I couldn't plead lack of time. And he had a full canteen, denying me the excuse of a parched mouth.

I told him of our adventure, pausing to drink and to soak the baby's pacifier every three or four sentences. She seemed to be enjoying what might have been her first ride in a jeep. During those pauses, Mwarai would verify the story-to-date with Basil, who was drinking while I was talking. The boy backed me every time.

I finished as we were crossing the plank bridge over the Nihuru. Once we were safely across, I tried to quiz the policeman about what had happened during our absence. He was still too mad to respond.

I found I was actually looking forward to my cell. To the bunk in my cell, to be precise. After a whopping bowl of *ugali*, I'd settle in for a nap that would carry me through the first half of my sentence.

Mwarai spoiled that happy picture by not taking me to the jail. We skirted the village entirely and headed north into the wooded hills. To Dr. Brocious's clinic, as it turned out. The doctor, who had been screening patients on his front porch, hurried down to greet us.

"So you brought them back alive, Chief Constable. Or should I say nearly alive? What in the world happened to you, Owen? And what's that you have? Raising a family and settling down, are we?"

He might have dithered on for another dozen stanzas, but Mwarai intervened. "That is another victim of the land violence, Doctor. Or so I am told. I require you to examine her and these other two as well. I will return for them shortly."

Brocious took up the baby expertly in one arm. In addition to a surprising sense of loss, I experienced a hot-poker pain in my shoulders and arms as I flexed my joints. And that was nothing compared to the experience of climbing down from the jeep.

Just shy of the clinic steps, I remembered a detail I'd forgotten to include in my report to Mwarai. I hobbled back down the sloped yard.

"Wait!" I called out over the whine of the jeep's reverse gear.

"What is it now?" Mwarai demanded.

"Do you know a Charles Njagi?"

"I do not. Why do you ask?"

Because a man who wore bed sheets had told me to. "Mugo gave me the name. I think Njagi has some connection to the land raiders."

When he got tired of staring me down, Mwarai repeated the name as I'd done for Mugo, jammed the jeep into first, and was gone.

By the time I got inside, Brocious was busy with Jane Doe. She cast what I interpreted as an imploring look at me, but the doctor wouldn't let me assist. He handed me a towel and directed me to his shower. "Make my job easier," he said. "Sluice off a little of that soil. I'm a doctor, not a farmer."

I looked for Basil on my way to the bathroom and found him asleep beneath a strange tree in the backyard. Its fragmented bark curled upward, making the trunk look like an unusually large bundle of peppers. Beside the boy slept a little yellow dog I'd not met.

If my elbows hadn't been on fire and the blisters on my feet had taken to the water better, I might have fallen asleep standing up in the doctor's galvanized tub. As it was, I outlasted the hot water heater. It hadn't come back by the time I found a venerable safety razor in the cabinet over the sink, so I shaved in cold water. It was wonderful.

I borrowed an extra large flannel robe next. This was after my very cursory medical examination. Brocious had lanced my intact blisters, daubed salve on the ones that had worn down to bloody skin, and pronounced me fit, tossing me the robe as a final test. I'd just managed to catch it.

"You're dehydrated, of course," he said. "So was the little tot. Dehydrated and half starved in her case. She's having her lunch right now, by the way.

"I expect you'll come down with any number of fatal diseases, but not before you've had a chance to tell me your story over a bowl of soup. Wait for me in my study while I find young Basil. He went out to play with my yellow pug."

I made my way to the book-choked study, settled into a chair, and immediately began to fight off sleep. It had been in every other thought I'd had for the past few hours, but I was afraid to give in to it now. Mwarai might burst in at any moment, or Gathitu. I should have been struggling back into my clothes, planning my next brilliant move. Instead, my head was lolling.

To keep it upright, I forced myself to examine the dusty books around me. A number of them were medical texts, but not as many as I'd expected. More numerous by far were works of history. African history and Kenyan history, but also histories of Great Britain and volume after volume on the Second World War. No surprises there. Brocious was a

Kenyan of British descent, and he'd told me he'd served in the war.

I noticed a little cubbyhole behind the doctor's desk, set directly behind his chair and so low in the wall that he'd blocked my view of it on my previous visit. The room's designer might have intended the space to hold a telephone or a statue or a trophy from the Somolet polo league, but like every other surface of the room, the recess had been given over to books.

I couldn't make out their titles from my seat, but that was all to the good. Moving my head alone was barely doing the job of keeping me awake until the soup arrived. So I struggled to my feet and circled the desk to have a closer look.

The little alcove held half a dozen volumes. All the titles were political, and only two authors were represented: Karl Marx and Friedrich Engels. I slid out a copy of *The Communist Manifesto*, remembering how I'd struggled through it back at Boston College in the wild sixties. This tiny edition had a leather cover, a rare thing in Brocious's library. The binding was worn thin with handling, and the pages were as well-thumbed as those of Swickard's breviary.

"One of the sins of my youth," the doctor said from the doorway. He carried our soup on a tray. "Political philosophy. Quite the thing at Cambridge in my day. Before the war, you know, when we still believed in political systems. I've moved from intellectual weaknesses to carnal ones as I've aged, reversing the usual order of march. Clear those papers off the desk. Throw them anywhere."

I returned the book to its place of honor and stacked enough of the papers on the ends of the desk to create an open space in the middle. In addition to the soup—chicken and rice that had lately resided in a can—the tray held some bread and two bottles of beer.

"Stout," Brocious said. "To help you ward off the dreaded Nihuru fever."

"Is there such a thing?"

He clinked his bottle against mine. "Why take the chance? Drink up and tell me how you came by our little guest."

"I thought you might know her name." It was an idea that had come to me in the shower.

"I? From having delivered her? I dare say I've brought my share of Kenyans into the world, but not this young lady. Childbirth is still very natural out here, for the most part. Especially at the remote *shambas*. I'm guessing this attack took place somewhere up valley, this being the first we've heard of it."

I did my best to describe the approximate location of the farm, as I'd done for Mwarai earlier. That had been an awkward moment, since it had also been the first time the chief constable had missed his map. Next I gave Brocious a description of the attack and of the woman I'd found behind the bench. When I finished, I noticed that my soup was untouched but my stout bottle was nearly empty.

The doctor was wiping his bowl with a bit of bread. We were seated across from one another, sharing the desk's kneehole. I watched his rubbery nose, its red veins just visible beneath his bloodshot tan, move up and down as he chewed the crust.

"We strike again, eh?" he said. "Man, I mean. What does the chief constable intend to do?"

"Look the other way, I suppose."

"Don't be too hard on Samuel Mwarai, Owen. If it weren't for him looking the other way, you'd be dining on something even less appetizing now, if you were dining at all."

"What do you mean?"

"Why do you suppose you're not under arrest at this very

moment? It's because Mwarai kept your absence secret from Karari Gathitu, the lord high executioner. Mwarai found out you'd taken off last night, when the major showed up looking for you. He's been protecting you ever since, at great risk to his career if not his neck. We're all just lucky that Gathitu hasn't been able to arrange your passage back to Nairobi yet.

"And don't forget who it was who found you out there and brought you in. If he hadn't, you might have been someone else's unappetizing lunch. That's not Hyde Park beyond the river. At any moment you might have attracted the attention of that lion we heard the other night. Then I would have been deprived of your company."

That gave me something to chew on besides the bits of rubber chicken. I was still at it when Mwarai joined us. He was carrying a bundle of clothes.

"I see you've worked another miracle, Doctor," he said. "My congratulations. Mr. Keane, I took the liberty of sending out to the lodge for a change of clothes for you."

Brocious looked from Mwarai to me and back again several times. Then he harrumphed something about having other patients to see. He closed the study door behind him as he left.

I spoke first. "I thought you might already be headed back across the river."

"To the site of the latest atrocity? I have sent a patrol. I could not go myself without attracting the attention of the commissioner."

And his displeasure. "Speaking of the commissioner's attention, thank you for covering for me while I was gone."

The policeman shrugged his narrow shoulders. "I was protecting myself as much as you. It would have gone hard for me if the man I had under house arrest had gotten himself eaten."

Something had softened his attitude toward me since our last meeting. Fortified by the stout, I decided to sit and wait for him to tell me what it was. After he'd moved his cap from hand to hand a couple of times, he did.

"I'm afraid our period of grace is over, Mr. Keane. I've just been informed that you are to be flown to Nairobi first thing in the morning. If there was something I could do. . ."

"There is," I said. "Get me in to see Philip Swickard."

## CHAPTER TWENTY-EIGHT

"And what do I say when it is reported to Commissioner Gathitu that you have left the lodge?"

When, not if. Mwarai was assuming that at least one of his men would let Gathitu know that I'd shown up in town. So I assumed it myself.

"Say that I asked your permission to take my leave of Father Swickard. I'm flying out in the morning. It's natural that I'd want to say good-bye."

"Perfectly natural," Mwarai said with decision. "Yes, I will take you to your friend."

I dressed, thanked Brocious, and said good-bye to Jane Doe, who was fast asleep. By that time, the chief constable had Basil in the idling jeep. The boy was scrubbed and sullen. He might have heard that I was leaving. Then again, he might have been down because Mwarai had confiscated his Bowie knife. It and Chesney's canteen were stowed between the policeman's seat and mine.

The run to Somolet was short, but I tried to make efficient use of it. "Any word on Charles Njagi?" I asked.

"I have initiated inquiries" was all Mwarai would say on the subject.

My first parting was not with Swickard. It was with Basil. As soon as we arrived at the police station, Mwarai called out for a constable. He handed the man the knife and told him to drive Basil back to the Bakaru farm.

"I apologize for depriving you of your companion, Mr.

Keane. But he's also the secret of your troublesome mobility. I cannot be sure of finding you when I want you as long as the boy is by your side."

We didn't have much time for our good-byes, but it was more than Basil cared to use. When I took his small hand and thanked him for his help, he responded by shaking his head in a rapid and continuous no. At the same time, tears welled up in his eyes.

I expected a much less touching exchange with Philip Swickard, given the way he'd lit into me at our last meeting. But he was too preoccupied to be insulting today. And not over his own situation, as I would have been in his place.

"It's started then, has it, Owen?" he asked as soon as I entered his cell. "The violence. I heard about the attacks beyond Agat."

"The violence started on your own front steps," I said.

Swickard then reminded me that he really had been out of the loop. "You can't believe the murder and the attacks are connected."

The priest hadn't risen from his stool. He was rumpled and unshaven, and his pale eyes blinked continuously, as though the soft afternoon light was overpowering them. I sat down on the bed without prior consent.

"Funny that you should mention my beliefs," I said. "I had an interesting chat on that subject with your friend Mugo."

"He came to see you?"

"No. I went to see him."

"*You* found *him*? How?"

"I let my fingers do the walking in the yellow pages."

Swickard winced. "Don't remind me of that, Owen, please. And please forgive me for calling you an idiot in front of Major Praed. I've had ample time to reflect on that. It was very wrong of me."

"You were wrong on another count. Mugo wasn't foretelling my arrival when he used the image of the hunter who doesn't believe in his prey. He was referring to someone else. Someone here in Somolet."

"He told you that?"

"Yes, but he didn't give me a name. Any ideas?"

Swickard put some effort into thinking, bowing his head until I could see a thinning patch on top. But he came up empty, or almost empty.

"I wonder if he might have meant me, Owen. I've often asked myself these past few years if my preoccupation with politics, with social justice, wasn't a sign that my faith in divine justice was waning."

His recessed eyes were fixed on me intently, and I realized that for once he was actually interested in my opinion. Owen Keane, the go-to guy on questions of waning faith.

"As a priest you have a responsibility for the temporal well-being of your people. Father Jerome told me that," I added, naming the old priest who had been rector of our seminary. He'd been the one who'd spotted that my own preoccupation with the worldly was a bad sign for my vocation.

Swickard must have gotten the same lecture. He said, "But Father Jerome also taught that a priest must maintain a balance between the temporal and the spiritual or he was lost." He looked around his little cell.

"Mugo's story wasn't about you, Philip. He told me it referred to someone in your acquaintance. Can't you think of any possibilities?"

"You've met my social circle, Owen. You give me a name."

"Could he have meant Wauki?"

Swickard ventured a thin smile. "Then it would have been the hunter who became the prey, though it isn't very charitable to joke about another human being's murder. No,

I don't see how it could refer to Wauki. Besides, I'd hardly say I was acquainted with him. What makes you think the hunter business is so important?"

That question brought me to a subject I'd been trying to avoid. "Daniel is with Mugo, Philip. He's there of his own free will. He would have left you months ago, only Mugo told him to stay at the mission and learn what he could from you."

"I see," Swickard said at length. He meant, "What next?"

I hurried on. "Daniel left when he did because Mugo had a feeling there was going to be trouble. When I asked him why he didn't warn you, he shot me an inscrutable smile. I think that smile meant that he had warned you, but not directly."

"Through the hunter image?"

"Maybe. What was the context of that? What had you two been talking about when he brought it up?"

"Everything, it seems. You've met the man. You know what a talker he is. He asked me questions about the mission and my background. But he would start in yammering again before I could get my answer out. We discussed transubstantiation, the Buddhist concept of the afterlife, the various translations of the Talmud. And it wasn't only religion. He touched on the rainy season, the seismic activity that had formed the Great Rift Valley, the advantages of maize over rice as a dietary staple."

"But what was the lead-in to the hunter reference? He couldn't have worked that into a discussion of crop rotation or annual rainfall."

Swickard did his hair-tucking routine as he struggled to remember. "He asked me about the Mau Mau uprising."

"Because one of the leaders had claimed to be the reincarnation of Wauki?"

"No. I don't recall Wauki being mentioned at that point. Mugo seemed to be interested in general information about the Mau Mau uprising. How it had affected the valley. Of course, I was still in school back in Indiana when all that happened, so I couldn't tell him much he didn't already know. I recommended that he try Rex Brocious, our local history buff."

Our friend the jailer arrived then to say that Mwarai wanted to see me at once. He emphasized the "at once" part by standing there at the cell door waiting for me to move. Mwarai might have been trying to warn me of Gathitu's approach. Even with that motivation, I dragged my feet.

"I was supposed to be saying good-bye to you, Philip. Now there's no time."

"It seems to me, Owen, that you left without saying good-bye back in seventy-three. Don't concern yourself about it now. I'm confident that we'll meet again, even if you're not." He peered at me while the jailer shuffled his feet. "You've changed, Owen."

"Since seventy-three? I expect so."

"I mean, you've changed since you arrived here in Somolet. You're not as shell-shocked as you were when you got off the plane. You're much more as I remembered you from the old days. What's caused that? What have you been up to?"

There was no time for a travelogue. "Hiking," I said. "It must agree with me."

Thinking back on 1973 had limbered up Swickard's memory. When I got as far as the other side of the bars, it kicked in again. "Owen, wait! I've just remembered something else. Mugo was curious about the power structure here in the valley."

"Chief Wamba versus Gathitu?" I asked, thinking back to something Major Praed had told me.

"No, not the visible power structure. A hidden, behind-the-scenes structure of power. Mugo seemed to be convinced that one existed."

I liked the sound of that. Unfortunately the jailer was reaching for my arm.

"Did he mention any names?"

"Yes, but you'll laugh when I tell you. He asked specifically about Elizabeth Chesney."

## CHAPTER TWENTY-NINE

Mwarai's summons had nothing to do with an impending visit by Commissioner Gathitu. I knew that the second I entered the chief constable's office. Mwarai was seated behind his junior partner's desk looking almost relaxed. Almost confident. He held a sheet of paper, which was blank on my side.

The policeman opened with a stall. "When you visited the Bakaru farm yesterday, did you speak with Etta the housekeeper?"

"No," I said, "just with Ruth the cook."

"You did not take the opportunity to verify your theory that a shirt of Father Swickard's had been stolen from the clothesline?"

"No." I'd needed that fact to be true, so I'd simply posited it as true, as I so often did.

Mwarai was mildly scandalized. "I visited the farm this morning, during my search for you. I questioned the housekeeper. A shirt did disappear, not on the day of the murder but a full week before. As the shirt was an old one and as Father Swickard is always giving things to those in need, Etta wasn't too concerned. What do you think of that?"

Just then all my thinking was taken up by the piece of paper Mwarai was teasing me with. "Did Etta write you a letter about it?"

He looked down innocently at the sheet. "This? This is not a letter. This a fax. From Nairobi. An amazing invention, the fax machine. You have one, of course."

"No," I said.

"My own is Japanese. A very dependable machine."

If Mwarai always got this chatty when he was relaxed, I preferred him edgy. "What did the fax from your dependable machine tell you?"

"It told me the identity of Charles Njagi. Think of that. I phoned in a request for information less than two hours ago and now I hold a report in my hand. Could the Scotland Yard of Great Britain do any better? I think not."

He waved the sheet in the air but still didn't offer it to me. "According to this, Mr. Charles Njagi was a small-time crook, a confidence man sometimes, a dealer in stolen goods sometimes. Not that interesting, you say. But there's more. Njagi sometimes did unofficial work for the labor ministry. His specialty was infiltrating labor movements and undermining their legitimate leaders. More interesting? You will find the technique he employed especially so. He would claim that the leader to be discredited was himself in the pay of the labor ministry."

That was very interesting. And very familiar. But I didn't want to steal his punch line. "You're speaking of him in the past tense," I said.

"Yes, I am. Charles Njagi is dead. His body lies not far from here, in fact. You knew him as the second resurrection of Chief Wauki."

He handed me the fax sheet at last. In its upper right-corner was a grainy photograph of the man who had died on the steps of the mission.

"I had the dead chief's fingerprints taken, of course, and sent by plane to Nairobi in an attempt to identify him. My request has not received a reply, has not even been acknowledged. My guess is, it never will be acknowledged."

"Because Njagi was working for the government again,"

I said. "Only this time, instead of discrediting labor leaders, he was going after critics of the land grab."

"Exactly. Father Swickard and Chief Joseph Wamba. But he used his old tried-and-true method. He accused them of being tools of the land raiders, when in fact he was the raiders' tool.

"Luckily you gave me a back door to go through by telling me of Charles Njagi. Evidently whoever placed the official roadblock in the way of my fingerprint request couldn't conceive of my ever learning Njagi's real name. A very efficient clerk faxed me a summary of Njagi's record, complete with the photograph we have both identified. I hope the clerk isn't made to suffer for that. Clerks always seem to have children. Many children."

I was scanning the fax. "It says here that Njagi really was a member of the Nihuru, but that he grew up in foster care in Nairobi. How did he get there?"

Mwarai performed another of his narrow-gauge shrugs. "We may never know. Young people of every tribe run off to Nairobi, sometimes because they are in trouble, sometimes because they are looking for trouble. Njagi's mother might have been one of those. That could explain how your friend the mystic learned Njagi's name. One of Mugo's contacts must know the truth of Njagi's background."

That sounded likely. But, as Mwarai's shrug had implied, it was also beside the point.

I asked, "How do we use this to help Father Swickard?"

The chief constable became considerably less laid-back, straightening himself in his seat and tugging the wrinkles out of his uniform shirt. "We cannot. None of this can help your friend."

"Because this proves that your government is behind everything?" In the absence of Major Praed, I was prepared to play the horse's ass myself.

Mwarai went easy on me. "You throw the word government about," he began quietly, "as though you believe the government of Kenya to be a single unified entity. It is not. I doubt that even in your country it would be fair to assume that the actions of one area of the government were known to all other areas."

"We have different levels of government, federal, state—"

"I'm not speaking of levels, Mr. Keane. I am speaking of factions. Forces within the government that are in competition with one another. At odds with one another. I am speaking of powerful individuals with their own followings, their own areas of influence, all struggling with one another under the leadership of one very powerful man, who has created the situation and remains in power because of it."

"More divide and conquer," I said.

"I would say divide and control," Mwarai countered. "But yes. So you see that simply saying the government is behind the raids does not advance us. But this new information is more troublesome for another reason. One that has more to do with our proper work as investigators."

"And that is?"

The policeman took the fax from my hand. "This strengthens the priest's motive for killing the impostor Njagi. That is what Commissioner Gathitu will say. He will say that the priest somehow discovered that Njagi was sent to discredit him, discovered that he was the priest's enemy, so the priest killed him. He will say that Swickard caught Njagi in the act of secreting the sword in the mission so that, as Wauki, he could enter the place and find it when the full moon came. So Swickard took the sword from him and hacked him to death with it."

"No one can say any of that without first admitting that

Njagi was working for the government," I said. Mwarai was shaking his head, so I edited myself. "I mean, some faction in the government."

That concession didn't stop the head shaking. "No one will be permitted to say that. The most that will be officially admitted is that Njagi was working for the land raiders. That will be enough to complete the case against the priest. Anyone, any defense attorney or policeman or private individual, who insists on tying those raiders to the government will end up in worse trouble than that very efficient clerk in Nairobi.

"So motive is one area in which this revelation works against your friend. But there is another. This information undermines your alternative explanation of the murder."

"How?"

Mwarai's rosy eyes were very sad. "You have said from the beginning that the land raiders were responsible, that by killing Wauki and framing Father Swickard for the crime they were silencing two critics with one stroke. Now we know that Wauki, Njagi, was their own man. Surely they would not kill one of their own."

"Njagi's done Swickard more damage in death than he ever did in life."

"Sadly that is true. But from the raiders' point of view it is just a fortuitous coincidence. A small compensation for the loss of their agent."

He consulted his watch. "I am afraid I am overdue to make a report to the commissioner. I will have you driven back to the lodge."

"I'd like to say another good-bye or two first, if you'll trust me one last time."

Mwarai's no was all but out of his mouth. He somehow held it in. "Good-bye to whom?"

It was a chance to test Mugo's theory that certain residents of Somolet had secret clout. One resident's name had worked on Mwarai before. It was worth trying again. "Elizabeth Chesney."

The regular squeak of the ceiling fan marked the passage of a long minute. Then Mwarai said, "It would be improper for you to leave without saying good-bye to a woman who has entertained you under her own roof."

He took the late colonel's canteen from a drawer of his desk and added, straight-faced, "You can give her this with your apologizes. I understand that you took it without her permission. Report back here when you are done."

## CHAPTER THIRTY

I'd noticed some bottled water in Somolet's little general store when Basil and I had had our ginger-beer break. I stopped in for some now. What I really needed was a more comfortable pair of boots. Or tennis shoes or snake-proof carpet slippers. The thought of walking to Chesney's cottage, which was just around the corner by Kenyan standards, had me limping like Tiny Tim.

The jumbled interior of the store revived the warm feeling of nostalgia I'd experienced on my first visit, when the place had reminded me of the New Jersey neighborhood groceries of my childhood, stores that had all since been eaten whole by supermarkets. Admittedly, there were some notable differences. Somolet's version had more exotic produce, and most of its dry goods were from Europe or Asia. And I couldn't remember ever seeing a fresh sheep's head on display in Trenton.

That sheep's head would have finished off my nostalgic mood single-handed if I hadn't happened to glance out the open back door of the shop. But I did glance out, and I saw a Volkswagen. I'd done a lot of my early work as an amateur sleuth in a VW of approximately the same mid-sixties vintage, a racy Karmann-Ghia with soggy rocker panels and taped upholstery. This one was a Beetle, a convertible that had lost its hubcaps, bumpers, running boards, and most of its sky blue paint. The folding roof was also gone, replaced by a rough wooden platform that covered the backseat and

200

extended out over the engine compartment. Making the old car the grocery's flatbed delivery truck, I decided.

The grocer, a man as old as the vagabond Tot but far more sedentary, had little English. Luckily one of the other customers was willing to act as translator. Through her, I asked the grocer how much he'd charge me for an afternoon's use of the Beetle. She gave his reply as "I will be honored to lend my car to a friend of the little priest."

The Beetle was right-hand drive, like every other vehicle I'd seen in Kenya, but I wasn't about to quibble over that. I climbed in, shook the gearshift lever for luck, and fired it up. The familiar lawn-mower sound of the engine was muted by the presence of the wooden platform, but it still tugged at my heart. I found first left-handed and roared off, troublesomely mobile once again.

I'd worked out many a puzzle while listening to the worn rattle of a VW engine. I had several new puzzles to work out now, courtesy of Swickard and Mwarai. Or rather, the priest and the chief constable had given me new pieces to work into a single puzzle, the mystery of Charles Njagi's death.

I started with Mwarai's pieces, having spoken to him last. He'd tossed off in passing the idea that Charles Njagi had come to the mission on his last night on earth to hide the Sword of Wauki. That made sense, if you assumed as I did and Mwarai did that Swickard hadn't taken the sword himself. In order for the priest to be completely discredited, the sword would have to be hidden in the mission for Njagi to find in front of as many witnesses as possible. It also made sense that the sword would be placed there as close to the full-moon deadline as possible, to lessen the chances of its being accidentally discovered by Swickard or Etta. Certainly it hadn't been there two nights before the murder, when the priest and I had searched the mission.

So Njagi had gone to the mission that night to hide the sword. How had he gotten it? Had it been passed to him on the night of Chesney's dinner party through those convenient French doors by one of her guests? Or given to him sometime later? Or none of the above?

I pressed down hard on the little brake pedal, and the car slid to a halt in the dust. I took it out of gear, but let the comforting engine rattle on.

I'd suddenly seen that Mwarai's insight also answered a question I'd been asking myself since the murder: How had the killer lured the phony Wauki to his death that night? That it had been prearranged for Njagi to die in that particular spot at that particular time I accepted as a given. The killer had gone to the trouble of obtaining and wearing Swickard's shirt, which meant the crime had been premeditated. The site had been selected, like the shirt, to incriminate the priest. So how had the murderer gotten Njagi to cooperate?

The answer again was the Sword of Wauki. Njagi had never had it. He'd gone to the mission that night to accept delivery of it.

Thanks to Mugo and Mwarai, I now knew that Njagi was connected to the land raiders. Unlike Mwarai, I still believed that the killer was also somehow connected to the raiders. He'd designed his crime, after all, to gag the raiders' most vocal critic. That the unknown had killed a fellow member of the conspiracy didn't bother me. He might have done it because, as the Praeds had told me, Njagi had proven to be a bust as Wauki, failing to rally any real support within the Nihuru. Or the motive might be something I couldn't see yet.

For the moment, I wouldn't let that distract me. It was enough to know that the killer and Njagi had been working together, up to a point. The killer's job had been to steal the sword and Njagi's to make use of it to embarrass Swickard.

It would have been the most natural thing in the world for the unknown to have arranged to deliver the sword to Njagi at the mission itself. So they could hide it together, two coworkers putting in a little overtime. That would explain the booming laugh Ruth had heard that evening. It had been Njagi's last laugh, perhaps in response to some joke his friend had made. After which, Njagi had turned his back to him and been hacked to death.

I patted the Volkswagen's steering wheel. It was the ivory color of the one in my old Ghia, but it lacked the imitation leather cover I'd sometimes used to give my car more sex appeal.

Everything about the killer's plan for that night had been based on the premise that the mission would be empty. So the killer had known that Swickard and I would be gone. Better still: He had arranged for us to be gone. He had to have done that even if he hadn't been planning to kill Njagi. The sword had to be hidden. Given the approaching deadline for its discovery, the conspirators couldn't simply wait for the right moment to come. They had to make it come.

I saw then that the killer had drawn Swickard away by first drawing me away. He'd sent Tot the vagabond to tell me of the sword in the remote *shamba*. I'd been slow to spot that story as the killer's work because Tot had been such perfect casting for the role of storyteller. Swickard had told me himself that Tot was exactly the kind of wanderer who would know of the existence of the samurai sword and exactly the kind of screwup who might confuse it for the Sword of Wauki. The other thing that had kept me from getting suspicious was my actually finding a sword at the *shamba*. That showed especially nice attention to detail on the killer's part. He could have sent me to any remote farm to get rid of me. But I would have seen right away that I'd been tricked. In selecting the Ngatini farm, the killer had gone a step beyond tricking me. He'd finessed me.

He might also have made the mistake of overreaching. By using the samurai sword, he might have given me a clue to his identity. I asked myself who among the people who had been in a position to steal the Sword of Wauki might also have known of Benjamin Ngatini's war trophy. I never got past the first name on my list: Elizabeth Chesney.

Her father had carried the samurai sword back from Burma and presented it to Benjamin Ngatini. And Elizabeth Chesney surely knew the Ngatini family, having been George's first schoolteacher. The old woman was an even better fit for the theft of Wauki's old cutlass. She certainly wouldn't have had to perform any sleight of hand during her dinner party. She could have taken the sword down from the wall on her way to bed that night. Hidden it in the root cellar or slipped it under one of the pieces of overstuffed furniture in her parlor. I might have been sitting right above it when she'd served me tea.

Chesney had the additional attraction of being one of the puzzle pieces Swickard had just given me. According to the priest, Mugo had asked about her in connection with his theory of a secret power structure in Somolet. I'd started out for the old woman's cottage in the first place to talk to her about that. Now I had other interesting topics for conversation.

Swickard had warned me that I'd laugh when he revealed that Mugo's secret mover and shaker was Chesney. I hadn't laughed. But now, as I got the old car moving again, I caught my reflection in the rearview mirror and saw the trace of a smile.

## CHAPTER THIRTY-ONE

When she greeted me at her cottage door, Chesney — very formal in her floral dress from the dinner party — shook my hand for the first time. Her grip was warm but not particularly strong, confirming what I already believed: She could only have wielded the cutlass through an accomplice. The attentive Norris Praed perhaps. Or the executioner might have been Reggie, her giant mastiff. The sight of him standing on his hind legs like a cartoon dog, swinging the sword in his teeth, could have been what had made the doomed Njagi laugh. Reggie looked like he'd happily use a sword on me if he had one handy. But, as usual, his mistress was all smiles.

"I heard about the little girl you saved, you and dear Basil. Word of it has spread through the village. You are to be congratulated, Owen. Heartily congratulated."

By then she'd led me into the parlor where we'd had our first interview, where I now hung the canteen back on its little hook on the wall.

Chesney eyed its soiled cover critically. "It wouldn't pass the colonel's inspection now, I'm afraid," she said. "But I think I know what he'd say of this dirt if he were here."

"That it's forever England?"

"No." She laughed almost girlishly. "That it was acquired in a good cause. A damn fine cause.

"Do sit down, Owen. And forgive my running on so. It may seem odd to you to applaud the saving of a single life on a continent where so many souls will die this year from

AIDS alone. But it *is* important. Every life is important. Each life is one more chance at an answer. A solution. An idea. An inspiration. A leader.

"If she does nothing else, this little girl of yours will be a representative for her dead family. How many families has this sad century seen erased in Europe and Asia and here in Africa without even one survivor to speak for all the lost?"

We passed a moment of respectful silence for those unknown dead. It gave me a chance to regroup, or try to. I hadn't been expecting all the backslapping from Chesney, and it had me doubting myself. Worse, when I'd decided to confront the old woman, I'd forgotten to take into account her very large dog. Somehow my relationship with Reggie had slipped another notch. As he watched me, he was impolitely licking his chops.

Chesney, on the other hand, was smiling full-time. It wasn't her mischievous smile either. I couldn't believe the smile was sincere, but I also couldn't detect a false note in her happiness or see the least contradiction of it in her eyes. The dog sat beside her, not reclining and not relaxing.

I said, "Did the local grapevine also tell you that I found Mugo?"

"No, but I guessed as much when I heard you'd visited the upper valley. I didn't think you would have strayed that far by accident. Not with Basil to guide you. What was your impression of the mystic?"

"That he wasn't what he appeared to be."

Now a trace of mischief shone through. "Who of us is, Owen? You, for example, are not quite the post-traumatic stress victim you seemed to be when we first met. Though I don't think I'd make that mistake about you today, if we were being introduced for the first time. You've quite changed."

"So I'm told."

"Of what did you and Mugo speak?"

"A number of things. He's quite the gabber."

"Anything that pertains to our troubles with the land raiders?"

That might have introduced Charles Njagi, but since I was sure that Chesney already knew—had always known—Wauki's true identity, I didn't waste our time with that. In fact, there was little that Mugo had said to me that I actually cared to share with her. Luckily, I had the mystic's earlier conversation with Swickard to fall back on.

"He had a strange idea about Somolet. He thought there might be a secret, unofficial structure of power here. And that you were a part of it."

"He said the same thing to Philip," the old woman observed, without getting the least bit ruffled.

I kicked myself for forgetting that Chesney's information about Mugo had all come from Swickard. She'd told me as much yesterday in her garden. I was unlikely to shock her with anything I'd gotten from the priest.

"What did you say when Philip told you?" I asked.

"I laughed about it. Philip seemed inclined to laugh, so I followed his lead. You seem to be taking it much more seriously. Is that because Mugo made a better case to you, I wonder, or simply because you don't know me as well as Philip thinks he does?"

I was experiencing something I hadn't previously in Somolet. A chill. I suddenly decided that the last thing I wanted, with Reggie sitting there salivating, was for Chesney to admit that she was behind the murder. To back us up a little, I improvised, using a stray detail from Swickard's chat with the mystic.

"Mugo also asked about the Mau Mau uprising. How it had affected this valley. Could some of the old Mau Mau

207

leaders still be alive and secretly exercising power?"

I was offering Chesney some cover, but she didn't take it. "No. Those who survived the British reprisals gained power quite openly when independence came. A few are still with us, but they're old men, enjoying well-financed retirements.

"Of course," she added conversationally, "there are some secrets connected with the uprising that have never been fully exposed. Will probably never be exposed. I remember the story of a renegade white who actually aided the Mau Mau, not here in the valley, but not that far away. Quite the scandal at the time, that a British settler would commit such a crime, though it was never more than a rumor."

"Man or woman?" I couldn't keep myself from asking.

"A man, in all the versions I ever heard. But then it would be a man, wouldn't it? In the rumors and legends, I mean, the popular imagination. It would take a rare thinker, an independent thinker, to suspect a woman of that treachery, especially in the 1950s."

Especially a woman who was a colonel's daughter. The daughter of the regiment. My attempt to draw Chesney back from a confession had backfired. But it had also gotten my curiosity salivating like the threatening dog.

"If this renegade were still alive," I said, "he or she might have connections to the government. At least to one or more retired members of the government."

"Or to the protégé of some retired leader," Chesney offered, nodding. "Yes, such a connection is certainly possible. Even probable. But it doesn't necessarily follow that it is an attractive or advantageous connection for the former renegade."

"What do you mean?"

She pushed a stray hair away from her face. Though dressed up today, she was wearing her thin hair down. "That this renegade has never been identified suggests to me, Owen, that he or she does not wish to be identified."

"Why would that be? From the renegade's point of view, the good guys won."

"It is a mystery. Of course, there were depredations committed by both sides during those troubled times. Our hypothetical renegade might have had something to do with one committed by the Mau Maus and been sickened by it, so much so that the sickness has lasted all these years. Then again, he or she might simply be disappointed or even disgusted with the government corruption that followed independence.

"For whatever reason, the renegade has kept a secret alliance secret, and that secret might be the renegade's weakness."

"Might be used to blackmail him?" I asked, using the masculine pronoun now not from old sexist habit but from a sense of self-preservation. My last attempt to keep Chesney from confessing until someone had clamped a muzzle on the mastiff.

"Yes," she said softly, "blackmail the poor old renegade into participating in yet another secret movement."

"The land grab."

I had everything I needed now. I had an explanation for the mystic's interest in Chesney. He must have a contact somewhere who knew of her secret connection to the Mau Mau. I also had an explanation of her involvement in the rotten land scheme. She was being blackmailed into it by someone in the government who also knew her secret, some Mau Mau veteran or the protégé of one.

Added to what I'd come with—a connection between Chesney and the samurai sword that had been used to lure me away from the mission—I had more than enough to present to Samuel Mwarai. If I could get to him. I tried to calculate the odds of reaching the French doors before Reggie sunk his teeth into me. It wasn't worth calculating. Even if I made it through the doors, I still had to reach the old car I'd left in the lane in front of the house. The way I was feeling, Chief Wamba could have beaten me to that.

I still didn't know why Chesney had turned on Njagi and arranged for his death. And I didn't know why she was being so forthcoming with me. Was she having a change of heart again, as she'd had with the Mau Mau? Was she so confident that Somolet was sewn up tight, so confident of her government backing, that she wasn't afraid of me or Mwarai or anyone else? If that were so, she wouldn't care whether I left or not.

There was an easy way to find out. I stood up on watery knees. Reggie immediately raised his slobbering head.

"I'd better get back," I said. "I was only supposed to be here long enough to say good-bye."

"Is it good-bye, do you think?" Chesney asked innocently as she tickled the dog's ear.

"Barring a miracle."

"Then we'll have to pray for a miracle, won't we? I suggest you return to the lodge and do that very thing."

## CHAPTER THIRTY-TWO

I did my praying in the Church of the Crucifixion, as it turned out.

I'd felt less safe walking through Chesney's flower garden to the Beetle than I had crossing the game lands with Basil. And the feeling hadn't gone away when I'd reached the car. It had all been too easy. I'd decided right then that I needed time to double-check my figures and that I needed to do it somewhere other than the lodge, the place Chesney had all but ordered me to go.

So I'd driven to the mission, ending up in the chapel, which, unlike the former great house, hadn't been locked.

The interior of the little building was very warm. For company I had some trapped flies and the contorted figure of Jesus over the altar. The carving wasn't comforting, but it also wasn't inappropriate. There was a certain similarity between the way the artist had arranged his subject on the twisted cross and the way Njagi had been sprawled across the mission steps by his murderer, except, of course, that Njagi had fallen facedown. There were other similarities besides composition. Both Njagi and the figure on the cross had been betrayed by someone they'd trusted. A follower, a friend. Who had Njagi's Judas been?

Once upon a time, I'd done more thinking in churches than I had in Volkswagens, though with less success. I found now that I was half sitting, half kneeling, with my head resting on the back of the pew in front of me. Fatigue, I told myself.

I reviewed my case against Chesney, finding one notable hole. It was that she had let me go off to search for Mugo. Had helped me go, in fact, when she could have stopped me with a phone call. And Mugo had given me the vital clue, the name of Charles Njagi.

Thinking of the mystic reminded me of his veiled warning about the hunter who no longer believed in his prey. If I was right about Chesney, the warning had to refer to her. But how? Because she had once believed in the Mau Mau cause but now didn't, though she was still serving their descendants?

Mugo had used the image after asking about the Mau Mau, or had he? I tried to reconstruct the order of topics Swickard had given me in those last few moments in his cell. Mugo had asked about the old uprising. Swickard had suggested he talk to the local expert, Dr. Brocious. Then Mugo had spoken of the hunter.

Brocious. The hunter allusion had been prompted by the mention of the Mau Mau and Brocious, not the secret power structure and Chesney.

I knew I was onto something at last. I looked up to the sufferer on the cross, half expecting a look or a wink of encouragement. But His eyes were still turned upward toward an unhearing heaven.

Brocious as the hunter who no longer believed in his prey. How might that work? What if Brocious was the white renegade and not Chesney? What if she hadn't been confessing at all when she'd told me that story, but pointing me toward Brocious in her fey, smiling way? Brocious was the right age to be the renegade. He was an expert on the Mau Mau, as Chesney had taken pains to point out to me during her dinner party. And he was a great lover of Kenya, though a disenchanted one.

The doctor was also, by his own admission, a former

Marxist. Could Mugo know that? If so, the prey he'd referred to, the prey Brocious no longer believed in, could be a failed political solution. "One of the sins of my youth," as the doctor had called his lost belief in social justice.

Brocious had been as well placed as anyone to steal the Wauki sword on the night of Chesney's original party. At one point he and Gathitu had been the only two people in the trophy room. I knew that because they'd alibied one another during our little game of Clue. And Gathitu was the man bent on railroading Philip Swickard.

All of my earlier suspects—Wamba, Mugo, and Chesney—would have needed an intermediary to have done the actual murdering. But not the doctor. As old as he was, he was still a big man. So big that he would certainly have had to leave Swickard's stolen shirt unbuttoned. Big enough to have delivered that first killing blow and all the wasted ones that followed. Brocious had described those subsequent blows to Mwarai and me as having come from pure hatred. He'd been testifying against himself then, and I hadn't seen it. He'd even planted the idea in Mwarai's head that the first blow had been struck by a short man, all the time acting the part of the reluctant witness.

Brocious had known to the minute when Swickard would be gone from the mission. The priest had phoned him and told him as much when he'd asked the doctor to join in the search for me. Which meant that Brocious had been the one who'd sent Tot to lure me away. Which meant in turn that Brocious must have known about the samurai sword. So there should be some link between the doctor and the Ngatinis that I could work out.

I'd no sooner set myself the task than I had the answer. It came in the form of a vision of Mai Ngatini waiting on us left-handed because she'd only recently had her right wrist removed from a cast. By a doctor who still made house calls. Brocious. It required no effort at all to picture the genial doctor sipping his *changa'a* and discussing the sword.

I had all Brocious's secrets but one: the reason he'd turned on Njagi and murdered him so savagely. Mwarai and I would just have to ask him for that secret in person.

That was my plan anyway. I closed up the chapel and headed for the Somolet police station as fast as the VW could carry me. But when I came in sight of the building, I saw a gleaming blue Land Rover parked in front of the station door. Commissioner Gathitu's official vehicle. I ducked my head, floored the worn accelerator, and roared straight through town.

Though the light was starting to fade, I was sure I could find my way to Brocious's clinic. I had no choice now but to try to tackle him alone. There was no safe way to contact Mwarai, no sure way to reach Praed, and my time was almost up.

I could easily explain a return visit to the clinic. I was saying my good-byes after all, and I had the added excuse of little Jane Doe. I'd have gone back to check on her in any case. It only remained to work out some way to finesse the doctor as he had finessed me.

I slowed the car to give me time to think and because I remembered the little elephant herd that Mwarai and Basil and I had dodged in that same stretch of woods. I was finishing my last downshift when a figure stepped into the road ahead of me. It was a man in olive drab fatigues carrying an automatic weapon.

Not now, I thought, though I might actually have shouted the words. I slammed on the brakes, shifted into reverse, and twisted in my seat. I saw a second armed man behind me, cutting me off as neatly as Mugo's scout had done on the forest trail.

Before I could even raise my hands, there were men at both sides of the car, closing the trap. The one on my side, who wasn't out of his teens, yanked open my door and pulled me into the road.

"I'm an American," I said.

The teen soldier didn't shrug at that or smile or spit. He kept a firm hold on my right arm, and one of his companions grabbed my left. Together they frog-marched me into the bush.

The trail we followed was only one man wide, but that didn't slow us down. Being in the center, I should have had the best of it, but I couldn't raise a hand to ward off the branches that came my way. I was cut about the face and bleeding when we reached a small clearing about a mile from the road.

There I was pushed down to my knees. "I'm a friend of Elizabeth Chesney's," I said in the hope her name would work as magically on my captors as it had on Mwarai. It didn't. I would have tried Brocious's name next or Gathitu's or Harry Ohlman's, but I didn't get the chance. One of the men taped my mouth shut while the other used a second strip to secure my wrists. The taping wasn't done gently, but I was buoyed by it. They wouldn't have bothered with bonds if they were planning to execute me on the spot.

Now that I was secure, we could walk single file in the fading light. I struggled to keep up with the man ahead of me, who was my only protection against the cutting under-growth. He set a pace that would have had Mugo panting.

After another mile we entered a second clearing, a larger one lit by the headlights of a truck. I had a glimpse of other soldiers before I went down again, this time flat on my stomach without anyone pushing me.

I'd almost caught my breath when a pair of boots arrived

in my field of vision. Highly polished black boots. As I was drawn to my feet by two unseen volunteers, I noted the newcomer's pressed trousers, the holstered gun on his belt, his uniform shirt devoid of any patches or insignia, and finally his face, with its scarred nose and bored expression. It was the man Basil and I had stumbled upon in the back garden of the burning farmhouse. The leader of the land raiders.

## CHAPTER THIRTY-THREE

The scarred man and I stared at each other for what seemed like an hour. In a movie, it would have been a natural spot for some bantering dialogue, something to show that the hero was still in charge of things, despite appearances. Luckily, I was gagged and Scarnose couldn't be bothered. When he finally did speak, it was in words I couldn't understand, addressed to the men holding me.

The man on my right released my arm to blindfold me, which sent my panic to a whole new level. When they dragged me backward, I tried struggling for the first time, now that it was useless to try. I heard one of the truck's doors slam very near me. Then a sound that could only have been the tailgate dropping. I was dragged toward that reverberating bang and lifted, kicking, into the air.

One of my kicks landed. My reward was to be tossed onto the bed of the truck so violently that all the wind I'd been fighting to recapture was knocked out of me in one go.

By the time I'd gotten a little of it back inside, the tailgate was up again, hard against my heels. I could both hear and feel the scrape of boots on the wooden floor of the truck, many pairs. I decided that a row of men was seated on either side of me, maybe six to a side, facing inward. Watching me struggle. Placing bets.

I trembled along with the floorboards as the truck's engine roared to life. The clunk of the transmission shifting directly below me was like a rap on my chin. Still, I was alive. I'd stay alive until we reached the raiders' camp, wherever that was. So there was still a chance.

Actually, the men flanking me weren't placing bets. I knew that because none of them was speaking. The only noise they made was an occasional grunt as the truck rocked and swayed. Desperate as I was for silver linings, I took heart from their silence and from my gag. If they were so worried about making a sound, about my calling out, they didn't feel safe. There was a chance we'd be stopped. I couldn't imagine who in Somolet would stop a truckload of armed men. But my captors could. That was enough for me.

Half an hour later I was taking a lot less comfort from my gag. By then I was getting nauseous from exhaust fumes coming up through the floorboards. I panicked all over again, imagining myself choking to death on vomit trapped by the strip of tape. I tried to roll over and got a boot on my back for my trouble. The truck slowed as I was pressed down by the boot, as though my spine had somehow become the brake pedal. Then the engine died.

It was too soon. The raiders couldn't be camped so close to Somolet. We'd stopped for some other reason. My juiced imagination supplied one immediately. They'd never been taking me to their camp. They'd intended to execute me from the start. They'd carried me this little way off so the shots wouldn't be heard.

The tailgate dropped with a bang I felt in every filling in my mouth. I was dragged across the rough boards, not dropped this time but set carefully down on my own two feet. As soon as I steadied, I knew I'd guessed wrong again about the raiders' intentions. This wasn't some deserted corner of the forest. I could make out lights through my blindfold. Many lights. And a dog was yapping not far away.

My guards steered me to my left and then lifted me. I

felt the tread of a step beneath my feet and got the message, climbing the next three without assistance. Once on top we crossed a plank floor that vibrated beneath us as the truck's bed had. Suddenly, the sound of our steps acquired an echo and the ambient light jumped. We were inside a room.

When my escorts released me, I swayed but stayed upright. Someone began sawing at the tape on my wrists. It parted, and I peeled my arms apart, anxious to remove my gag. That was already being seen to.

"Gently," a voice I knew said. "That's right. The blindfold as well."

Then I was blinking in the light of kerosene lanterns at three people seated shoulder to shoulder. The one in the center was no surprise; I'd already recognized her voice. To Elizabeth Chesney's right sat Norris Praed. To her left, Samuel Mwarai. The three of them, in league with the land raiders. I swayed again.

"Get Mr. Keane a chair, Okola."

The man Chesney addressed, who was holding my blindfold and my tape bonds, was Scarnose himself. He was the only one of my captors still in the room.

Okola did as the old woman had ordered, retrieving a folding chair from a pile of them and setting it behind me, hitting me with it on the back of the knees so hard that I sat down involuntarily.

"Thank you," Chesney said. "Now you may go."

Okola marched out without a word. I heard the truck engine start as soon as the door to the room had closed behind him.

I thought about bolting for that door while the three of them sat there like a review board considering a very unpromising cadet. Mwarai and Praed were wearing side arms, but those didn't stop me. What stopped me was the challenge of rising from the chair.

We were in a barracks-like room that was vaguely familiar. It was the twin of the infirmary where Chief Wamba had
shown Mwarai and me the attack victims, except there were
no beds, only stacks of folding chairs and tables. So we were
in Agat, in some kind of common room.

Praed spoke first, perhaps because I happened to be looking at him just then. I'd been noting that his eyes had lost
their tired look.

"Jesus, Owen. Is it your standard operating procedure to
just waltz into the killer's house unarmed and ask him for
the story of his life?"

I'd done it so often, intentionally and unintentionally, that
it could have passed for a standard procedure. Or at least a
very bad habit. But Praed wasn't expecting an answer.

"Lucky for you, Okola was keeping an eye on the doctor's
place. Otherwise Brocious might have killed you ahead of
schedule."

That last remark was jarring, but it didn't quite undo the
encouraging tone of what had come before. Praed was berat-
ing me, but as one team member chiding another. Mwarai's
opening remarks were in the same vein.

"It was very brave but very foolish, Mr. Keane. You've
been fooling the doctor right along, I know, but it wouldn't
do to beard the old lion too often."

"Fooling him?" I managed to ask.

Mwarai took the question as a criticism of his English.
"Handling him. You suspected him from the start and never
let him know. Not even when you pointed me toward him that
night at the mission, when you observed the very sharp edge
someone had put on the old cutlass. With all due respect to
the major, I knew that edge had not been done by any farmer
at his grindstone. I searched the doctor's clinic when he was
out making his rounds. In the machine he uses to sharpen

his instruments, I found some very peculiar filings, as you knew I would. They will be positive proof of the doctor's guilt when they are tested."

Good old Mwarai. I was always going to be the great detective for him, blindfolds and gags and sweat-stained shirts notwithstanding.

Chesney was tighter with her praise. "I had my doubts as to whether you had correctly identified the doctor. But you did snap at the lure I cast you. The story of the white renegade."

I'd snapped at that lure twice, once for her and once for the doctor, as I suspected she knew. But she didn't call me on it.

"It was Brocious, of course," Chesney said, in clipped speech very out of keeping with the Miss Marple character she'd been playing for me. I'd already noticed that she'd stopped addressing me as Owen. And smiling. The men on either side of her were listening with respectful attention. She was still wearing her party frock and should have seemed out of place. Instead, she was the focal point of the room.

"He was living some way east of here back then, in the Great Rift Valley itself, a young idealist with his head full of nonsense about enslaving mankind in order to save it. He's much wiser now, for all the good it does him. His past associations are well known to Karari Gathitu and to Gathitu's superiors in Nairobi. They feel free to call on him for any odd job that strikes their fancy."

"And he just goes along with it?" I asked.

"He has no choice," Chesney replied. "He knows that at the very least his masters can expose him as the long-ago traitor, which would cost Brocious a social position he's come to value, ironically. He's more British than communist, in the last analysis."

"But why would these masters order the murder of Charles Njagi? He was their man, too."

"Murdering the false Wauki was Brocious's own idea. He must have done some pretty fancy explaining since, as he's still alive."

## CHAPTER THIRTY-FOUR

Praed stood up and slipped into a shadowy corner of the room as Chesney continued her lecture.

"Njagi must have known the doctor's secret. That made him a dangerous man, from Brocious's point of view. Njagi had fallen in love with the part of Wauki, as I'm sure you noticed when you spoke to him. And he was failing at it, which made him desperate. He may have threatened to take the doctor down with him, so the doctor acted to save himself."

Praed reappeared at my elbow with a cup of water. "Drink this, old sport," he whispered.

Chesney's voice took on the slightest hint of asperity at this interruption. "Brocious went to his elaborate lengths to cast blame on Father Swickard in an effort to save his own neck. Gathitu and the others were given the choice of revenging themselves against the doctor or eliminating a troublesome priest. They chose the latter."

I'd tried to sip my water slowly, but it was already gone. "You're certain that Gathitu is behind the attacks?"

"Yes."

I tested the cuts on my face with the back of my hand. None of them seemed too active. "How do you know for sure? And how do you know so much about Brocious's past, if it's such a secret?"

Mwarai and Praed both stirred and both made a point of not looking at Chesney, who didn't stir. She said, "To explain our knowledge of the doctor's past, I must trust you with a secret of my own, Mr. Keane. Once, before independence came to Kenya, I had the honor to serve as a very minor operative of British Intelligence. As such, I had access to all information on the white Mau Mau, as we called him. We suspected Brocious, but we lacked the evidence to act. Then independence came, and there was no reason to act."

"So Mugo was right about your being a member of a secret power structure."

"Yes and no. I haven't been an active member of any intelligence service for many years. The power structure the well-informed Mr. Mugo alluded to does have a connection to my secret past, but only a very tangential one."

"My favorite kind."

Chesney almost smiled. "How can I explain this as simply as possible? I was, as you know, a school teacher. As such, I had a hand in shaping generations of young Kenyans. One of my former pupils has gone on to do quite well for himself. He is, in fact, a highly placed minister of the current government. The chief constable has explained our peculiar form of government to you, I understand. It sometimes seems to me to be analogous to the European kingdoms of the Middle Ages, with a group of rival feudal lords all loyal to a single powerful king. My former student is a member of one of those rival factions. Gathitu and his superiors belong to another.

"I know the Gathitu group is behind the land seizures, to answer your earlier question, because my former student has told me so. Gathitu's cohorts originated the scheme in the northern districts. Now it is our commissioner's turn to benefit from it. His plan is to enrich himself, to reward his followers with grants of land, and eventually to undermine and eliminate Joseph Wamba.

"When Mugo asked after my secret connection to political power, I suspect that he was searching for some means of countering Gathitu and his faction. As it happens, I had already thought of asking my friend in Nairobi for his help."

"And he happily risked his neck for you? You must have been one hell of a school teacher."

But not one that liked her students speaking out of turn. Chesney made me wait a beat before answering me.

"That is where the tangential connection to my work for British Intelligence comes in. It would embarrass and even damage my successful pupil were it to become known that he'd been mentored by a British agent. In exchange for my silence, he is willing to do an occasional favor for me."

"Gathitu doesn't know about your secret past?"

"No. He only knows I have a powerful friend in Nairobi and therefore cannot be trifled with. He doesn't know the true basis of that friendship. He must never know."

She stared that point home before continuing. "Mr. Okola, whom you've met, and his men were sent by my friend to look into the attacks. Okola was fact-gathering when you saw him at the burning farm and mistook him for one of the raiders."

"Why didn't he do something to help?"

"Because he's a more dispassionate observer than you are, I'm afraid." Chesney showed her age then. "What were we discussing?"

"Our organization," Praed said.

"Ah, yes. Prior to Okola's arrival, I'd enlisted Major Praed's help and Chief Wamba's. This afternoon the major invited Chief Constable Mwarai to join our coalition, and he bravely accepted."

I was suddenly feeling braver myself. "Wait a minute. You had all this up and running before you let me go out searching for Mugo. Why didn't you stop me and tell me what was going on?"

Chesney consulted her watch. "Your chief value to us has been as a diversion, Mr. Keane. A distraction for the chief constable, before he joined us, and for Commissioner Gathitu. I thought if you were to disappear it would throw the commissioner off balance, buy us further precious time to organize. That didn't happen, as it turned out, because neither the chief constable nor Dr. Brocious, who also knew you were gone, informed Gathitu. They both chose to protect you. That was one of the things that convinced us to extend our invitation to Samuel Mwarai."

"What about Brocious? Why would he protect me?"

"He's not a bad man, Owen," Praed said. "He just picks the wrong sides. Or has them picked for him."

"He's a murderer," I reminded him.

"He lashed out when he was cornered," the major said. "Any animal will do that."

I said, "I left the baby with him."

"She's perfectly safe," Chesney said, without a trace of her earlier enthusiasm for the subject of Jane Doe. "She poses no threat to anyone. You are quite another matter. Your expedition into the bush has had an unforeseen benefit for us. You witnessed the attack on the farm. What is more, you returned here and talked of witnessing it. That has increased your value to us enormously."

She took a well-deserved breather, allowing me to live up to Mwarai's high opinion of my brain power by working out the rest. Thanks to the major's earlier crack about Brocious killing me ahead of schedule, I found that I could.

"You need me as bait in some kind of trap. You don't expect Gathitu to let me live, now that I'm a witness to an attack. But I didn't see that much at the farm. The only one I can identify is Okola."

"The commissioner does not know that," Mwarai said and

looked away guiltily. I saw more of Chesney's handiwork in that look. She must have rewritten Mwarai's report to Gathitu. In her version, I'd probably seen everything but the raiders' birthmarks.

Praed said, "It'll be like setting out a goat to catch a lion. He'll come for you tonight. It has to be tonight because the whole village knows you're flying out tomorrow. We'll snug you back in your hut at the lodge and wait. When Gathitu and his gang show up, we'll have them."

"What makes you think Gathitu will dirty his own hands?"

Chesney answered. "He daren't trust Brocious. The doctor's nerve is gone. And I don't think he will trust another accomplice. Not after the troubles Njagi and Brocious have caused him. No. This time, he'll act directly."

I found my feet at last. "Why don't you just go get him? You've got your own little army."

"So has Gathitu," Chesney said. "The land raiders. We have our support in Nairobi, and so has he. A balance of power exists, and we need something to unbalance it. Gathitu's arrest by Chief Constable Mwarai for your attempted murder and his confederate Dr. Brocious's arrest for the murder of Charles Njagi will tip things our way. We will spare the people of this valley any further violence. And we will save Philip Swickard."

They had me and they knew it. The plan was Swickard's best hope. Even if I decided to desert the priest, my only way out of the valley was the commissioner. The man who would never let me go.

"If Gathitu kills me, your case against him will be airtight."

This time Chesney did smile. "It will do us no harm to hope."

## CHAPTER THIRTY-FIVE

I was sweating again. I noticed that as soon as Praed got his
Land Rover moving and the cool night air hit my shirt. The
major was even cooler than the slipstream, to judge by his
happy chatter.

"What'd'ya think of her Owen? She's a treat, isn't she?
An iron lady if ever there was one. Don't let her fool you
with all that 'minor operative' stuff. She was something of a
legend, was the colonel's daughter. Back during the big war,
I mean. She was working in occupied France then and just
out of school. Some of the stories she told me about those
days gave me gooseflesh. I guess she got pretty handy with
a garrote toward the end. I haven't felt safe with my back
to her since I heard that." He laughed as though he'd told a
great joke. "If only half her stories are true, she's a woman
to reckon with."

I thought Praed was probably right to add that caveat.
Since the stories had been intended by Chesney to impress
Praed and secure his help, there was no telling how much
sawdust they contained. Still, the major was obviously smit-
ten. If Chesney had been a few decades younger, Lori Praed
would have had a serious rival. And poor Lori had looked to
Chesney to help keep her husband out of trouble.

"Did you notice how she glossed over her little blackmail
operation? Her old friend the minister in Nairobi is only too
anxious to do her the odd favor in exchange for her silence.
So like a Brit. She makes it sound as though they worked it

all out over their afternoon crumpets. The truth is she's got his balls in a mangle and she's happily turning the crank. You can bet she's got the goods tucked away somewhere safe, to be opened in the event of her death. Otherwise, Okola and his beauties would be on her trail, not Gathitu's."

I decided that Praed was more keyed-up than I'd first thought. He was prattling on like Mugo after his second cup of tea.

"Speaking of Okola, I'm sorry he bounced you around so hard, Owen. I don't think he likes you. He heard that description you gave of him in your report to Mwarai. Guess he must think that scar of his is scarcely noticeable."

Picturing Okola and his scar lit by the flames of the farmhouse reminded me of someone else who'd been there. I grabbed Praed's arm.

"What about Basil? He saw as much as I did. If Gathitu is eliminating witnesses, he'll go for Basil, too."

"Relax. Her nibs thought of that. Your little sidekick is somewhere safe."

We were climbing the false escarpment by then. Praed downshifted as the grade steepened. As he did, he lowered his voice until I could just hear it above the straining engine.

"Okola and his men will be in place by now. We just need to drive in and act natural. Can you think of any funny stories?"

"No," I said.

"Me either. Guess we'll just play it straight and sober."

That would be hard for the ex-soldier. He could barely keep from grinning, the idiot; this was so much more fun than playing innkeeper.

Lights were burning in several buildings of the lodge, but no one was in sight. "Told the help to lie low but to light the place up. Keeps the animals away, if you know what I mean."

Praed drove me right to the door of my cottage. Then

he walked me inside. For the benefit of anyone who might be watching, he banged me on the back as we followed the stone path, congratulating me in a loud voice for saving the baby girl. He ended the speech with "That calls for a drink."

The whole damn day did, I thought, but I didn't say anything. The major was overacting enough for both of us.

Once inside, Praed unsnapped the cover of his holster and had a look around. I did my looking from the center of the circular structure. I could see that the place had been tidied up. And that my dirty laundry had been stolen. Luckily, the thief had overlooked the bottle of scotch Praed had brought me on the night of Njagi's murder.

I crossed to the table the bottle shared with an empty ice bucket and a pair of tumblers and poured two drinks. Praed joined me then, having checked for assassins everywhere but under the bedspread.

He'd forgotten his earlier suggestion that we drink to Jane Doe's delivery. "What's the toast then, Owen?"

"Success to crime," I said from old habit. I was hoping to confuse the major and maybe even wipe the grin off his face, but I was underestimating the reach of American culture.

"Humphrey bleeding Bogart. *The Maltese Falcon*," Praed said, grinning even more maniacally. He rammed his glass against mine and emptied his in a gulp. Then he got serious long enough to make me a dumb-show offer of his pistol. I shook my head, and he holstered the black thing again, snapping it in tight.

"Have a good night then, Owen," he boomed as he marched to the door. "I'll get you to the airstrip in the morning, no worries."

I stood there with my glass in hand, listening to the Land Rover making the short trip to the lodge proper. A minute later I heard Praed closing the lodge door behind him, slamming it, in case Gathitu's spies were deaf. The trap was set.

I checked the imitation bamboo dresser and found my missing clothes, all washed and ironed and folded. I laid out a complete ensemble and then started the shower going. Praed the old movie buff would have been making references to Alfred Hitchcock and Janet Leigh if he'd been handy, but I felt safe under the steaming water. As the major himself had observed, nothing much was going to happen while the lights of the lodge were burning.

Afterward I considered improving on the shaving job I'd done at the clinic and decided against it. The cuts I'd collected while breaking trail for Okola's henchmen had gotten tender all over again in the shower. I checked them in the bathroom's misty mirror, then moved to examining the face behind the cuts. It was an older face than I'd expected to see. An older one than I was used to seeing. But then, I hadn't been paying close attention lately.

I dressed, found the glass of scotch I still hadn't tasted, and went to the window that looked toward the main house. No lights were visible anywhere around the lodge property. Praed was hurrying things along. I decided I'd keep my own lights burning till dawn and realized that wouldn't help me. If mine were the only lights, they'd be a beacon for whoever was coming for me.

I compromised with my wiser self, switching off all the lamps but one, a zebra-striped table lamp next to my one-bottle bar. I dragged a chair into its circle of light and settled down to drink. I wasn't even tempted by the bed, though it had been forty-eight hours since I'd slept in a real one and I hadn't done a great job of it then. There'd be time for a long sleep later, I told myself. One way or the other.

It was the perfect moment for introspection. The Johnny Walker alone should have ensured that. A New Year's Eve moment, one made for lamenting past failures and making hopeless resolves for the future. Only a day earlier, I'd been resolved not to have a future. And yet I'd struggled against Okola's men. I could have tried to solve that puzzle as I sat drinking. Instead, I found myself thinking of a certain doe-eyed baby, wondering what would become of her. That reminded me of what Chesney had said about every life being important because each one represented another chance at an answer. I couldn't be sure if Chesney, the Spider Woman of Somolet, really believed that. It didn't matter anyway. I believed it at that moment, alone in a hut in the wilds of Kenya. And my wait was eased by it.

The knock on the door was so soft I was almost able to convince myself that I hadn't heard it. Then it came again. I struggled to my feet, calling out, "Who's there?"

The reply was little louder than the knock. "Basil."

Little Houdini had slipped his bonds again. And again he'd escaped from relative safety straight into the lion's mouth.

I hurried to the door and slid back the bolt, the first words of a reprimand on my lips. Where they died. The sight of Basil, standing there as frightened as he'd been at the burning *shamba*, would have been enough to shut me up. But he wasn't alone. Behind him stood Karari Gathitu, the muzzle of his automatic pistol pressed against the boy's head.

## CHAPTER THIRTY-SIX

Gathitu was wearing a very plain cap and vest tonight. They were a blue bordering on black. Almost mourning attire. His mood didn't match the ensemble. He was grinning like Praed had, so much so that the little goatee on the end of his jutting jaw seemed to be curling upward from the strain.

The grin was frightening, but it took second place to his eyes. For the first time, I was seeing him without his gold-rimmed sunglasses. His eyes were a glittering brown and almost without pupils. In contrast, Basil's pupils were dilated hugely in the weak light of the entryway. The commissioner was high on something besides the thrill of cornering me.

"You will not keep us standing in your doorway surely, Mr. Keane. That would be a violation of good manners. Even of what passes for good manners in your barbaric country."

I backed into the room, and Gathitu pushed Basil after me. Once he had closed the door behind them, the commissioner gave the boy another shove, sending him across to me. Basil took my hand.

"Very touching," Gathitu said. "But then you two have been through so much together."

"The boy didn't see anything last night."

Gathitu shrugged. "He has seen much tonight. He will see more shortly."

He looked around the pretend hut. "Quite a nice room. If only you'd come back here yesterday as I ordered you to do. You might have lived to see your America again.

"But then you wouldn't have solved the mystery. And for a detective, the solution is all."

My only chance was to keep him talking until Praed and the cavalry showed up. They were taking so long about it that I half-believed Chesney wanted a smoking gun in the commissioner's hand. I forced myself to look away from the window and back to that hand and its gun.

"You have your priceless solution by now, do you not, Mr. Keane? You know that Dr. Brocious is the murderer."

"I know that he isn't the murderer. He was only the murderer's instrument."

I hadn't exactly said the first thing that popped into my head. I'd expressed a nagging doubt that had been bouncing around in there since Chesney's lecture. Gathitu's pinpoint eyes flashed with interest.

"Whose instrument?" he asked.

"Yours, of course."

"Oh no, Mr. Keane. Dr. Brocious acted without orders. He felt threatened by Njagi, threatened with exposure and the loss of his place in our happy little community. He cast blame on the priest in a desperate effort to save himself."

He'd summarized Chesney precisely. I spotted that on some level and felt a warning tingle, but I was caught up just then in our give-and-take.

"Brocious isn't a killer," I said. "He's still sick about the killing he saw in the war and what the Mau Mau did and what was done to them. He wouldn't have killed Njagi to save his good name. He would have run first. That's what he's always done. He ran to Kenya from England after the war. He ran to this valley after the Mau Mau were beaten."

"Then why didn't he run this time?" Gathitu asked. "Why didn't he run instead of carrying out the orders you say I gave him?"

"To save his own life. You had him cornered and he knew it. It was Njagi or him."

I saw it all then. Those unnecessary hate-filled blows that Njagi's corpse had endured hadn't been directed at him at all. Not really. Brocious had been striking at Gathitu, the man who had made him a murderer. The man he couldn't touch. I understood why Brocious had covered for me and why he'd spoken so feelingly about the pressure Mwarai was under. I even understood why Gathitu had come for me in person. Chesney had been wrong about that, just as she'd been wrong about the reason the doctor had killed the false Wauki.

"Your being off in Nairobi the night of the murder, the night the sword was to be hidden in the mission, was too big a coincidence," I said. "You arranged to be gone to give yourself an alibi. You ordered the murder. And you instructed Brocious to frame Father Swickard for it. You were happy to trade a failing operative for a chance to knock Swickard out of his pulpit. There'd be one fewer voice to tell the world what was going on in this valley."

"Bravo, Mr. Keane," Gathitu said, bowing his regal head. "Really fine work. I regret now that I didn't have the witch Chesney brought here to witness you in your glory. It would have made her defeat total if she'd been made to listen to her solution being topped by that of an American amateur."

The warning tingle I'd felt earlier became a full-fledged tremor of alarm. Gathitu saw it and bowed again.

"Correct, Mr. Keane. You needn't glance at the window again in the hopes of seeing Major Praed. That bull-necked man has been subdued. Surprisingly easily, I might add. Oh yes, his annoying bluster is quite gone now. That lovely wife of his would hardly recognize him.

"To save you the pain of any more false hope, I should add that it is also beyond the power of the other conspirators to help you. As I implied just now, Chesney has been taken at long last. So have those who were foolish enough to place their trust in her, Joseph Wamba and the traitor Samuel Mwarai. The chief constable has been executed by now on my orders."

I heard a truck climbing the grade to the lodge. As did Gathitu.

"What's that you are thinking?" he asked eagerly, the glittering eyes flashing again. "That I have omitted a name from my list? That there is still hope? That the vehicle you hear might carry your savior and his men? Again I must disabuse you. Okola, Chesney's mercenary, has come over to my side. In fact, he has been on my side for some time. He didn't like taking orders from an Englishwoman. And his former superiors in Nairobi did not pay him adequately. I was in a position to offer Okola land, the preferred currency in Kenya. He is coming for you now."

Actually, he'd arrived. The truck had stopped somewhere very near, probably in the very spot where Praed had parked earlier.

"So you see, there really is no hope. Philip Swickard will be tried and convicted for the murder of Charles Njagi. And you, Mr. Keane, will simply disappear. Your death will be a mystery, as befits a famous detective. One last mystery to end all mysteries."

Or the answer to all mysteries, I thought. At the very least, it was the answer I'd come to Kenya seeking. I suddenly knew I didn't want it.

"I don't want to disappear."

"I beg your pardon."

"I don't want to die in Kenya."

"Do you imagine, Mr. Keane, that you have a choice?"

"No," I said. "I just wanted it on the record."

Gathitu bowed one last time, as though granting me that boon. I immediately moved on to another.

"What about the boy?"

"He chose his side. Now we will go out. You two will proceed me."

Though Basil still clung to my hand, he didn't hold back as we started for the door. He still had faith in me, I realized. He still expected me to save him somehow. The thought made my despair complete.

The truck was parked where I'd been picturing it. It was a canvas-topped military transport without markings. Probably the truck that had carried me to Agat.

I hesitated at the cottage threshold. A man had stepped from the shadows to stand on the path between the cottage and the truck. Okola, smiling at me, his arms folded across his chest.

"Proceed, Mr. Keane," Gathitu said from inside the hut. "Don't falter now."

I started forward, scheming desperately. Okola wasn't holding a gun. None of his men was in sight. And Gathitu was high on something. If I turned and threw myself at him, Basil might be able to slip away in the darkness. I squeezed the boy's hand and released it. He seemed to read my whole plan in that squeeze. He kept his hand raised but didn't grasp mine again.

Just as I started to wheel about, I heard Gathitu scream. I finished my turn in time to see Samuel Mwarai wrench the automatic from the commissioner's hand. One of Mwarai's constables had Gathitu in a neck lock.

I wheeled again to face Okola. He hadn't moved, hadn't even unfolded his arms.

"Easy, Owen," a voice called out from the darkness. "He's on our side. But he might just break your neck for practice." Praed stepped into the light. He held a rifle across his chest, and one of his eyes was swollen shut. "Got him there, Samuel?"

In reply, Mwarai said, "Karari Gathitu, I arrest you for the attempted murder of Owen Keane."

And the murder of Charles Njagi, I thought but wasn't able to say. It could wait.

The policemen led the struggling commissioner past me, Mwarai intoning his rights. Okola finally moved, stepping over to the truck and drawing back the canvas cover. Rex Brocious was seated within in handcuffs, his head bowed.

"What's going on?" I asked.

"Our trap has sprung," Praed said, patting Basil on the head. His swollen eye made his happy grin a steady wink. "A mite more elaborate a trap than the one Elizabeth described to you. We were all the bait, her nibs and me and Mwarai and old Joe Wamba and you two. Elizabeth arranged for Okola to contact Gathitu and pretend to betray us. It was the only way Okola and his men could operate in the valley without risking a big firefight with the raiders. We let Gathitu think we were all in the bag tonight. So he'd drop his guard and come for you personally."

"Why didn't you tell me?"

"'Why worry the goat?' was how the old girl put it. I would have dressed it up a bit, but then you know what a diplomat I am. Any of that scotch left?"

## CHAPTER THIRTY-SEVEN

Early the next morning, I was reclining on the little patio that
overlooked the man-made pond that overlooked the Nihuru
Valley. I was waiting for my orange juice to be delivered on
a chilled tray by a beautiful woman. It promised to be quite
a wait, since the woman in question—Lorelei Praed—had
only just been recalled by her husband and couldn't possibly
arrive in Somolet for another day. I made up my mind to sit
right there and keep watch for her.

The rising sun was rising behind me, fortunately, because
I had the ghost of a hangover and I'd lost my Nairobi hat
when I'd been ambushed by Okola's men. Not that I could
escape that powerful sun entirely. Out beyond the shadow
cast by my cottage's conical roof, the sunlight was glinting
off the pond water, forcing me to close my eyes from time
to time in self-defense. After one particularly long bout of
this eye resting, I looked out beyond the shimmering water
and saw Mugo.

He was posed there like a sleeping crane, his arms folded
so that his white shawl covered him to his knees, his head
bowed. He was greeting the sun perhaps or saying one
morning prayer for each of the many religions he hoped to
reconcile. If so, he was going to be at it until long after my
orange juice arrived.

He wasn't at it that long, of course, because what he'd
really been waiting for, huddled there in his cocoon of brilliant white, was for me to open my eyes and be impressed. I

239

did, I was, and so he unfolded his arms and circled the little pond to join me.

I got up on bare blistered feet and moved the chair I'd been saving for Lori Praed a few feet to the left so it was out of the cool shadow of the cottage and in the full sun. I knew the mystic wouldn't pass up the chance to glow. I was less sure that he would grant himself the luxury of a chair.

At first he wouldn't. He stopped some little way off and said, "I was just performing a very ancient morning ritual, an unspoken prayer to the rising sun. The supplicant spits on the palm of his hand—or blows on it if he prefers—and holds the hand out toward the sun. The origins of the practice are lost in time—may be as old as time—but the sense of it seems to be 'Again this day I offer up my spirit to God.' I was taught it by a relatively untainted tribe, whom I think of as a living link to my ancestors."

"Our ancestors," I said.

Mugo considered me with a tilted head. Then he crossed to the chair I'd set out for him and settled in it quite naturally. First though, he did something more surprising still. He shook my hand.

"I have come to offer my congratulations, Mr. Keane. My very sincere congratulations on the successful conclusion of your dangerous struggle. I had received word—another of my intimations really—that last night would be the climactic night. I was nearby as a result, but moving in the shadows as is my wont."

He sounded embarrassed over that. He was awkward in general this morning, but then this was our first meeting since he'd deserted Basil and me at the burning farm.

To let him know I wasn't holding a grudge, I said, "Thanks for telling me about Charles Njagi. I'd still be lost without that."

Mugo bowed his head in acknowledgment. He wasn't ageless now, in the full light of day. I decided he was sixty, which made the chase he'd led me through the forest even more remarkable. More *ugali* in the future, I thought, and fewer bacon cheeseburgers. It was one of many resolves I'd made that morning by the little pond.

"You have heard the latest developments?" Mugo asked.

"Haven't even had my orange juice yet."

"Then I have the pleasure of reporting that the raiders—Commissioner Gathitu's raiders—have all been gathered up in Elizabeth Chesney's net. And that our friend Philip Swickard is safely back at his mission house. I was surprised to learn that you were not with him."

I was a little surprised myself. I'd accepted Mwarai's assurances that he would release Swickard without delay, but I hadn't gone to see it done. I'd told myself that I'd earned a little solitude, something hard to come by at the mission. But the truth was I expected my reunion with the priest to be far more awkward than this meeting with Mugo was proving to be. Not because of the things he'd said to me in anger in his jail cell. The awkwardness would all be on my side. I'd started underestimating the little priest back in our seminary days and never really gotten past it. Until now. Now I saw his life, his example, as an indictment of the way I'd wasted the past two years. Of the way I'd spent the last twenty.

Mugo was still patiently waiting for his answer. I said, "I expect I'll move back to the mission today."

"Good. Father Swickard intends to celebrate a service of thanksgiving at noon. I am reliably informed that it will be very well attended. Many Nihuru who are not of the father's faith will be there to show their happiness at his release. I will be there myself, though perhaps at a little remove. Will you come?"

"Yes," I said.

"Very good. It will be a fist in the eye of the forces of non-belief for so many of different faiths to gather together."

"Who are these forces of non-belief?"

Mugo beamed to match his sunlit robes. "Your curiosity regarding intangible, impractical things is returning? Excellent. But I do not know the answer to your question. If I did, my quest would be over. Yours would be as well, I think."

"Mine may be over anyway," I said, thinking of one of the many resolves I'd made that morning.

"I would be sorry to hear that," the mystic said, rising from his chair. "You must decide, of course. And I must be content with the knowledge that the reports I have received of you since your return from my forest are true."

"What reports?"

"That the dark girl, your constant companion, no longer follows you. I came here this morning to verify it for myself. I am happy to say that she is truly gone.

"Go in peace, Owen Keane."

I did go in peace, but not for several days. Swickard insisted that I stay on to see what ordinary Kenya was like. That gave me a chance to say a real good-bye to the people I'd met, including the beautiful Lorelei Praed. Her long-looked-for return was a little disappointing, as her absence had made her fonder of her husband and vice versa. The only time I saw her without the major in tow was when she came to the mission to meet little Jane Doe, whom Swickard had added to his extended family. The baby's real name was Song, which we learned from her uncle and aunt, traced by the industrious Samuel Mwarai. Until her relations showed up, I had the pleasure of Song's company every day. I felt a real pang the evening she and her uncle and aunt drove off in Mwarai's jeep.

When the priest finally tired again of having me underfoot, he arranged for my flight out. On the appointed morning, he drove Basil and me to the airstrip using the rutted cliff-top road. On the highest bluff, he parked the jeep with its square nose pointed toward the river and the rolling brown game lands and the distant blue mountains of Tanzania.

"Thought you might like one last look at that wilderness," the priest said. "Though I don't suppose you'll ever forget it. And I wanted one last chance to say something I've been trying to say for days."

"You've already thanked me."

"It's not another thank you, though God knows I owe you a round dozen. No. I wanted to apologize."

I'd been on the brink of my own apology many times over those last days, but I'd never made the leap. Now Swickard leapt for us both.

"I wanted to say I'm sorry, Owen, for dismissing you as I have for so many years. For dismissing the way you've chosen to spend your life. I can see now that what you've chosen to do is far from easy. And that it has value."

I'd received affirmations from unlikely sources before, once from a man who couldn't remember what he'd had for breakfast and more recently from a drug-induced figment of my own imagination. None meant more to me than Swickard's grudging concession, made there above the muddy Nihuru.

"I wish I'd chosen your path, Philip."

He gently amended that. "I wish you'd been able to."

My last good-bye was said to Basil, beneath the wing of Noah's venerable Cessna. In the course of it, the boy dug into the pocket of his shorts and extracted a flat red stone, highly polished.

"For me?" I asked.

"For the girl who drove the boat."

It took me a moment to recall the story of the haunted cannery. "For Amanda?"

"Yes," Basil said shyly. "For Amanda."

"Don't grow up too fast," I said.

I took off my private eye hat, which some kind soul had found on the seat of the old Volkswagen delivery truck, and placed it on Basil's head. He immediately tugged one side of it down, like a Kenyan Dick Powell, and grinned at me.

He was waving the hat over his head as we climbed away to the east.

## ACKNOWLEDGMENTS

Owen Keane depended on his guide book in Kenya, and I leaned heavily on one in writing this book. In my case, it was *Traveler's Kenya Companion*, Allan Amsel editor-in-chief, Anne Trager editor. A second book that was indispensible to me was *Nine Faces of Kenya*, a collection of writings about Kenya compiled by Elizabeth Huxley. I would also like to thank Sheryl Hemkin for reviewing the manuscript and correcting some of my imaginings.

# AN OWEN KEANE CHRONOLOGY

The following chronology lists all Keane short stories, novellas, and novels in order from Keane's point of view and gives the year in which each tale is set. For the actual publication order and years of the novels, please see the list at the beginning of this volume.

(Some titles will be unfamiliar even to faithful readers of the series. These are as yet unpublished cases.)

| | |
|---|---|
| 1950 | Keane is born in Trenton, New Jersey |
| 1967 | "St. Jimmy"* |
| 1969 | *Orion Rising* (Flashback Story) |
| 1973 | *The Lost Keats* |
| 1976 or 1977 | "The Judas Clue" |
| 1978 | *Die Dreaming* (Book One) |
| 1981 | *Deadstick* |
| 1981 | "Main Line Lazarus"* |
| 1983 | "The Headless Magi"* |
| 1984 | "After Cana" |
| 1986 | *Live to Regret* |
| 1988 | "The First Proof" |

| | |
|---|---|
| 1988 | *Die Dreaming* (Book Two) |
| 1989 | "The Triple Score"* |
| 1990 | *Prove the Nameless* |
| 1990 or 1991 | "The Incurious Man" |
| 1993 | *The Ordained* |
| 1994 | "The Third Manny"* |
| 1994 | "On Pilgrimage"* |
| 1995 | "The Seven Sorrows" |
| 1995 | *Orion Rising* (Contemporary Story) |
| 1997 | *Eastward in Eden* |
| 1997 | "The Widow of Slane" |
| 2001 | "A Sunday in Ordinary Time"* |
| 2002 | "Ghost Town" |
| ???? | "Will and Testament" |

\* Collected in *The Confessions of Owen Keane*

## ABOUT THE AUTHOR

Terence Faherty is the author of two mystery series: the Shamus-winning Scott Elliott private eye series, set in the golden age of Hollywood, and the Edgar-nominated Owen Keane series, which follows the adventures of a failed seminarian turned metaphysical detective. His short fiction has won the Macavity Award, and has been nominated for the Anthony, the Barry, and the Derringer awards. Faherty is a member of the Baker Street Irregulars and an occasional lecturer on the films of Basil Rathbone. He lives in Indianapolis, Indiana, with his wife Jan.